MW00456973

HARD RAIN

THE COLUMBIA ORAL HISTORY SERIES

Edited by
Mary Marshall Clark
Amy Starecheski
Kimberly Springer
Peter Bearman

Robert Rauschenberg, edited by Sara Sinclair with Peter Bearman
and Mary Marshall Clark

HARD RAIN

*Bob Dylan, Oral Cultures, and
the Meaning of History*

ALESSANDRO PORTELLI

Columbia University Press

New York

Columbia University Press
Publishers Since 1893
New York   Chichester, West Sussex
cup.columbia.edu

Copyright © 2022 Columbia University Press
All rights reserved

Library of Congress Cataloging-in-Publication Data
Names: Portelli, Alessandro, author.
Title: Hard rain : Bob Dylan, oral cultures, and the meaning of
history / Alessandro Portelli.
Description: New York City : Columbia University Press, 2022. |
Series: The Columbia oral history series | Includes index.
Identifiers: LCCN 2021040204 (print) |
LCCN 2021040205 (ebook) | ISBN 9780231205924 (hardback) |
ISBN 9780231556231 (ebook) | ISBN 9780231205931 (paperback)
Subjects: LCSH: Dylan, Bob, 1941—Criticism and interpretation. |
Dylan, Bob, 1941-. Hard rain's a-gonna fall. | Folk songs—
History and criticism. | Ballads—History and criticism. |
Music and history. | Lord Randal.
Classification: LCC ML420.D98 P68 2022 (print) |
LCC ML420.D98 (ebook) | DDC 782.42164092—dc23
LC record available at https://lccn.loc.gov/2021040204
LC ebook record available at https://lccn.loc.gov/2021040205

Columbia University Press books are printed on permanent and
durable acid-free paper.

Printed in the United States of America
Cover design: Noah Arlow
Cover image: Alamy

CONTENTS

HARD RAIN

INTRODUCTION

MEMORY, VOICE, AND THE GLOBAL BOB DYLAN

ROME, ITALY: TURN OFF THAT AWFUL VOICE

"A Hard Rain's A-Gonna Fall" is the first Bob Dylan song that was ever aired on Italian radio. I know because I was the one who played it. This book—a study of the relationship between Bob Dylan's masterpiece and a traditional ballad known as "Lord Randal" in the English-speaking world and "Il testamento dell'avvelenato" ("The poisoned man's testament") in Italy—is the result of an obsession with this song, its roots, and its ramifications that has been with me for more than half a century and has traced the development of my work from folk song to oral history as ways in which the popular classes give voice to their relationship to and presence in history.

So let us begin with memory. Greil Marcus, one of Dylan's most perceptive critics, asks: "Everyone remembers where they were when they heard that Kennedy was shot. I wonder how many people remember where they were when they first heard Bob Dylan's voice."[1] I remember very well.

My journey toward folk music, oral history, and Bob Dylan began in the late 1950s with the Kingston Trio's pop-folk version of the Appalachian murder ballad "Tom Dooley."[2] In 1960, while spending a year as an exchange student in a Los Angeles high school, I bought all the Kingston Trio albums I could lay my hands on (I still have them, and I still find them respectable)[3] and discovered slightly more sophisticated groups like The Limeliters,[4] almost forgotten today, but important in the folk music revival. My liberal school mates introduced me to my first Pete Seeger album; after I returned home for Christmas in 1963, they sent me the Peter, Paul and Mary album *In the Wind*, an intriguing mix of British popular ballads and African American numbers held together by the trio's elegant sound. What made it exciting, however, was the last track, a mysterious song called "Blowin' in the Wind," with its haunting melody and thrilling lyrics. I checked the disc's label to find out where it came from and found only one, cryptic word: "Dylan."[5]

That same Christmas, my American "sister" Melody Hinze sent me the album of a then-unknown folk singer from San Francisco, *The Best of Joan Baez.*[6] Back then, Baez didn't even seem to have enough songs to fill an album, and some of the tracks were handled by now forgotten partners Bill Wood and Ted Alevizos, but the voice was already stellar. A couple of years later, a friend came back from the States with another album of hers, *Joan Baez in Concert*. Once again, we were enchanted by her voice. But what amazed us was one of the tracks, a song about the war history of the United States, from the Native

American genocide to the Cold War, always in the name of God. The title was "With God on Our Side," and the label only carried the same, laconic word: "Dylan."

Back then, traveling to the United States was expensive and difficult, and folk records had no Italian distribution. I was working in an office at the National Research Council, so when my boss went to a conference in the United States, I begged him to get me anything he could find about this mysterious Dylan. He came back with a gray record sleeve with a picture of an odd asymmetric face, and a prophetic title: *The Times They Are A-Changin'*. When I got home, I put it on (on the wrong side), and out came an unbearable voice that told a terrible story: "A bullet from the back of a bush. . . ."[7]

I was still living at home, where I had established the elegant voices of Peter, Paul and Mary and Joan Baez as the soundtrack of daily life. But Dylan was something else. As soon as I put the record on, my father broke into my room shouting, "Turn off that awful voice!" I brought home the works of Mao Tse Tung and the autobiography of Malcolm X, but the only thing to which my father ever objected was the sound of Bob Dylan's voice. I, too, had to learn to like it, just as at about the same time I had to learn to appreciate the voice of Giovanna Daffini, the great traditional singer from Emilia, another one who did not sing to please.[8] Since then, I no longer care for pretty voices.

It was Bob Dylan, who named Woody Guthrie as his inspiration, who gave me the courage to invest 10,000 lire, about fifteen dollars then, 30 percent of my first paycheck, on two Woody Guthrie and Leadbelly vinyls (the latter was probably the same that someone had given to sixteen-year-old Robert Zimmerman in 1958). I remember hesitating by the racks at a downtown record store: "What if I don't like them?" I finally decided that if I wanted to be serious about all this, I had to try, and I took the plunge. I came home, put Woody Guthrie on the record player—"I'm gonna hit that Oregon trail this coming fall"—and that voice has stayed with me for the rest of my life.[9] The next step, of course, was investigating whether there was such a thing as Italian folk music, discovering there was, listening to the folk singers' stories, and moving on to oral history from there—but that is another story.[10]

Woody Guthrie wrote once, "None of the folks I know have got smooth voices like dew dripping off the petals of the morning violet . . . I had rather sound like the ashcans of the early morning, like the cab drivers cursing at one another, like the longshoremen yelling, like the cowhands whooping, and like the lone wolf barking."[11] This is the quintessential American voice—the gravelly voice of Louis Armstrong, Little Richard, Almeda Riddle, Tom Waits, Blind Willie Johnson. And Bob Dylan. In my Bob Dylan imprinting, songs like "Only a Pawn in Their Game" or "The Lonesome Death of Hattie Carroll" were shocking for the racist crimes they exposed, chilling for their insight into the souls of the murderers, and "surprising" (Greil Marcus's word) for the strident sound of Dylan's voice. Today, that voice is familiar and canonical, but that voice at that time was a break from all we had heard before.[12] At that time, learning to appreciate that voice was not only an aesthetic, but also a political and moral lesson. And it wasn't just me, either.

NEWCASTLE, ENGLAND: "YOUR SONS AND YOUR DAUGHTERS ARE BEYOND YOUR COMMAND"

January 2018. An oral history talk in Newcastle, England, Ken Loach country, in the once industrial and coal-mining Northwest. In my lecture I mentioned Bob Dylan; when it was over, a member of the audience approached me and told me a story. Fortunately, I had my digital recorder on.[13]

My name is Terry Hilton. I live in Sunderland, come from a working-class family. The way I was introduced to Bob Dylan was my eldest brother, John, who died unfortunately at the age of forty-three. I was around fourteen and fifteen, somewhere round about that; and he came in one year with an LP by, I didn't know who it was at the time of course, the man was called Bob Dylan, and it had a number of songs from Bob Dylan. The song I really remember the most was "The Times They Are A-Changin'," and it was electrifying, it was a kind of music that you wanted to stand and think about what's going on in the world, what's happening, all the changes that the man was singing about.

My father had two hundred years of mining history behind him. He was a typical working-class lad, he was hard working; when I recorded his life story, I was shocked to hear some of the things that he said. For example we always thought—we came from a Catholic family, there was nine of us in the family—and we always thought our father went down the pit because his father died and he was his mother's help, you know? But two years before me dad died,

I interviewed him and I asked, "Why did you go down the pit?" And he said, "Well, when I was a kid growing up in Wingate, in a pit village," he said, "you had two ways of being a man." He said, "You went to a grocery shop, and you worked in the shop," he says, "or you went down the pit like your father did." He said, "All them that went to a grocery we thought of them as thots,[14] as . . . as effeminates. And every-[thing] I wanted to do was be like me dad. I really wanted to go down the pit, I wanted to be like me dad." But [then he said]: "No more; none of my children are going down the mine," so we had to find another way.

My brother never went down the pit because me father insisted that none of his children, none of his boys ever went down the pit. John was ahead of his time as a teenager. He was like—very early sixties. And all of us were kind of normal schoolchildren, normal things and everything. He was like radical, he would wear pin-striped trousers, he wore velvet trousers, I mean, can you imagine a young man like seventeen years or whatever the age at that time walking around a working-class street in Sunderland with pajama-stripe trousers on? He stood out like a sore thumb, you know? At the time that this was happening, of course, we were [seeing] images of things that were happening in America, where young people were in revolt against the established order and, to cut a long story short, all of this developed into a kind of naive rebellion, probably one of the first rebellions in Sunderland of its kind, because it led into drugs, the drug scene.

John got involved in all of that, and I eventually got involved in that as well, although I kept a wide berth, you know, but I was fascinated by what was going on at the time and the whole of that period was cued by music, music that had absolutely massive effect in our lives at that time. I mean, we listened to rock music, it went on from Bob Dylan. From Bob Dylan it went into the Velvet Underground from America, it went into other bands in England. We went to see some of these bands live and music was very strong, there was a drugs scene going on, it was the first time that drugs hit Sunderland and we felt as though we were kind of like, hanging in a new kind of culture at the time, you know? I saw some of what was going on; I didn't like what was going on, I experimented with the drugs then I pulled my foot back, I said this is not for me.

You know, I can't listen to Bob Dylan without crying because it reminds me of all the memories of my brother who I looked up to. He was my big brother and I looked up to him. He had more going for him than I ever had, I used to ask him questions [and] he used to give us the answers. So when I listen to Dylan, it kind of reminds me of that a lot, because I lost him when I was so young. John, me brother, he had a brain like me dad, he was the best educated of our family, he passed his elevens, he was a grammar school boy, he was top of the class, and he was doing really well at school. So when he kind of changed with his Bob Dylan thing and the new music that swept through us at that time, and the culture that went with it and the drugs that came with it, and the dress and everything, the long hair, the strange dress, I mean he was quite a leader of his own group, he was a rebel, he was against authority, he ended up in . . . for a little while, and that wasn't very pleasant for him, he spent three weeks in . . . a petty crime, that was a petty crime, but he was a leader of his own class, and people followed him and looked up to him and everything, like I did. So I well remember the Bob Dylan era.

SONG AND/AS ORAL HISTORY

This book did not originate as an oral history project, but inevitably it gravitated in that direction. I suggest, however, that as we read this book, we seek another connection between "oral" and "history": going beyond the standard oral history practice of using interviews to reconstruct and interpret past events and their meaning, and listening to the other forms of oral expression in which the popular classes have perceived and represented their historical presence and agency. This book, then, is a multidisciplinary investigation on history and memory through the prism of the primary orality of folklore, the secondary orality of mass media, and the conversation between them, based on a specific case study.[15]

Bob Dylan was part of the original impulse that led me, through Woody Guthrie and the working-class partisans of the Gramsci Brigade, to folk song first, and to oral history later. From the very beginnings of the Italian political and intellectual tradition from which I come, as represented by activist scholars like Gianni Bosio and Cesare Bermani, folk song and oral history were never separated but always connected and intertwined as sources for the history, memory, historical presence, and self-representation of the working classes. The Italian folk song revival, indeed, was as much the work of historians like Bosio as that of anthropologists like Alberto Cirese and musicologists like Roberto Leydi.[16] All of my own oral history work begins with music. Dante Bartolini's songs "Vile Tanturi" and "Il 17 marzo," about a partisan battle in 1944 and the killing of factory worker Luigi Trastulli in 1949, together with the complicated narratives that accompanied them, set in motion half a century of oral history work in Terni, Italy. I would not have spent thirty years on an oral history of Harlan County, Kentucky, if I hadn't been motivated by songs like Florence Reece's "Which Side Are You On" or Sarah Ogan Gunning's "I Hate the Capitalist System."[17]

In more recent times, the same approach has been extended through the growth of "cultural studies" to popular culture as historical source; thus, "Lord Randal" and "Hard Rain" will be treated here both as texts *in* history, documents of their time, and as texts *about* history and its meaning. And, since we are dealing with poetic works, the multidisciplinary approach also entails a good deal of textual and literary analysis.[18]

In this introduction, I use oral history interviews from Italy, England, and India, as well as my own memory; as is often the case with oral history, the "historian" is also part of the story. Cultural and oral historians have long been aware of the value of music and song as repositories of the folk memory of historic events and forms of history-telling.[19] The relationship of song and memory as a record of specific historical events is underlined by the incipit in several songs of Terni's working-class bard Dante Bartolini: "Non ti ricordi ancor del 10 marzo"; "Non ti ricordi mamma quella notte" (don't you remember March 10, a partisan battle in 1944; don't you remember the night the Fascists came, in 1922)—or Woody Guthrie's ballad on the great Los Angeles flood, "Oh friends do you remember, on that fatal New Year's night. . . ."[20] The historical meaning of music and song, however, goes beyond topical reference to individual events. Dylan's refusal to admit that "Hard Rain" is about the Cuban missile crisis allows the song to resonate in time toward the past and the future. In this way, while the song gives voice to a generation's concerns toward what history had in store, it remains relevant in the face of new and future dangers. In this book, the resonances of "Hard Rain" from the time of its writing to the present are set in the context of the memory and oral histories of contemporary social movements and events, from the generational discovery of state violence in Genoa in 2001 to the wave of migrations across South-North borders in the United States and the Mediterranean.

As I will argue in the following chapters, "Lord Randal" / "Il testamento dell'avvelenato" is about time, the dangers of uncontrolled change, and the hope of resilience and survival. Taken together, and enriched by their reciprocal resonances, these ballads and Dylan's song generate a powerful metahistorical reflection about time, change, and the meaning of history. Metahistorical, however, does not mean ahistorical. The folk life of "Lord Randal" spans the *longue durée* of the rise and demise of modernity, and its variations across the century turn it into a palimpsest of historical continuity and change. By grafting his song onto the cultural memory of the ballad, Bob Dylan in turn extends its *longue dureé* into a vision of the future—and, in the same gesture, as we shall see, radically alters its meaning.

Both oral history and folklore are arts of balancing, in their own distinct ways, the individual and the social. Oral history recognizes memory and narrative as deeply personal constructs and expressions that are yet shaped by social, cultural frameworks and in turn change them, somehow in the same relationship as *langue* and *parole* in post-Saussurean linguistics. In different forms, these dynamics occur both in "Hard Rain" and in "Lord Randal." On the one hand, an individual author's deeply personal creation becomes the shared property of multiple generations in many continents. It stands as a "representative" text not because it is average, but because it is unique. Like Emerson's "representative men," all major works of art, and the uncommon stories of certain oral history narrators, "Hard Rain" explores the range of what is historically, culturally, socially *possible* and conceivable at a given time and place.

On the other hand, a song and a story of obscure origin and "authorship" like "Lord Randal" is shared in social collective memory, but survives in different epochs and cultural environments thanks to the myriad individual changes generated by countless individual performances and personal recollections; an "archetypical" and apparently ahistorical text becomes, through the sum of its variations and versions, a movable social history of family and social roles in the West.

These processes are the result of distinct forms of artistic creation. Bob Dylan's song becomes a kind of collective property thanks to the mass reproduction and distribution of cultural industry, in the shared ceremony of the concert as oral, musical, and multimedia performance, and in the personal memory and imagination of millions of fans. On the other hand, "Lord Randal" is, like all folk song, the temporary result of countless individual interpretations in performance of a socially shared "text." These different processes also generate different poetics, based on the different forms of the polarity and dialogue of orality and writing. Part of what makes Bob Dylan special is the way he positions himself at the crossroads of these different forms of creation and poetics, bridging orality and writing, performance and text, folk tradition and modernism, topicality and prophecy, history and archetype. Ultimately, in their distinct and yet converging ways, both "Hard Rain" and "Lord Randal" stand, individually and together, as explorations of continuity and change, history and time, apocalypse and survival. This is what the chapters to follow are about.

ROME, ITALY: IT AIN'T ME, BABE

I kept on stockpiling American folk music records and playing them for my friends. The brother of one of them was radio personality and jazz critic Adriano Mazzoletti. He had never heard that kind of music and offered me a spot—I could play one record a week—on his program on the flagship channel of national radio. The first song I played was "A Hard Rain's A-Gonna Fall." In the following weeks, I introduced the program's audience to Pete Seeger ("Little Boxes"), Joan Baez, Tom Paxton ("What did you learn in school today / Dear little boy of mine? / . . . I learned that our leaders are the finest men / And we elect them again and again"), Phil Ochs ("We're the cops of the world"), and Simon and Garfunkel's "The Sounds of Silence" ("The words of the prophets are written on the subway walls, tenement halls . . .").

Back then, very few people in Italy had heard about Bob Dylan—indeed, hardly any that I knew of. Legend (and unreliable oral sources) has it that he had been in Italy in 1962 and had appeared at Rome's Folk Studio, where they did not seem to realize who they were dealing with.[21] It was only in 1966, at a concert of the Nuovo Canzoniere Italiano, an activist folk music outfit founded by Gianni Bosio, that I heard Rudi Assuntino, a pioneer of Italian protest song, present his translation of Dylan's "Masters of War." "I had heard two kids sing 'Blowin' in the Wind' on the beach at Brighton," Rudi recalls. "I was with a friend, and we hardly knew any English then, but we asked them to write the words down for us, and painstakingly translated them when we got home."[22] For years, there was no campfire on Italian beaches without a solemn choir ("like in church," a young German tourist commented once at a campsite in Calabria) of "Blowin' in the Wind."

In 1966, I was working on my first book, an amateurish but sincere anthology of American folk and political songs.[23] The publisher wanted me to secure the rights for each text I was planning to include, and it turned out that Italian rights for Bob Dylan's songs were held by Vincenzo Micocci, a major record producer. Micocci told me that he could not authorize me to use them; he asked me, however, if I could do singable Italian translations of Dylan's songs for a young Neapolitan singer he had just discovered named Edoardo Bennato. Bennato would later become a major pop-folk-rock star on his own, but in those days he was just a young kid with a guitar and a homemade harmonica holder. He would ride from Naples to my house in his purple convertible, and we would spend hours toiling on Italian texts for Dylan and Donovan (the only one I remember writing was a version of "Love Minus Zero/ No Limit"). At some point, we thought that we might as well write our own songs, and I wrote a couple of Dylan-ish texts that Edoardo recorded on a soon forgotten 45 rpm, for which I still get about five euros' worth of royalties a year. My military service and Bennato's booming career drove us apart, and I never got around to asking him where he had first heard of Bob Dylan.[24]

It has been more than half a century since then, and Bob Dylan, 2017 Nobel laureate, is still a protagonist of our time. All this time, he has meant different things to different generations. I was born a year later than he was, and I first heard him in 1963. Like Terry Hilton, the singer-songwriter star Francesco De Gregori—a Bob Dylan fan and translator of his songs—learned about him from an older brother:

I was about 15, must have been in 1966 or so. I had been fascinated by Peter Paul and Mary's "Blowin' in the Wind," until one day my brother [Luigi Grechi, also a musician] came home with a 45—I remember the gray sleeve, a gaunt young man's face—and told me: this is how it should be played. For me, it was the sound; I was already of the generation for which the important thing was the sound.[25]

Silvia Baraldini (1947), a revolutionary activist in 1960s America, never heard Dylan until *Nashville Skyline*.[26] Alessandro Carrera (1954), Italy's finest Bob Dylan scholar and critic, and one of the best all around, writes, "I have been listening to Dylan since 1970."[27] Writer Alessandro Robecchi (1960) fills his witty and brilliant crime novels with Dylan quotes and references that I have to look up because none of them belong to the Dylan I grew up with. Marco Rossari (1973), author and translator, first heard Dylan in 1979; he bought his first album, *Oh Mercy*, in 1989.[28] Gaia Resta (1979), a teacher and also a translator, encountered Dylan as late as the mid-nineties:

> I was fourteen when I discovered Dylan, and it was a revelation, from some TV program where they played excerpts from what I later realized was the Rolling Thunder Revue Tour. The camera focused on his face, and it's hard to explain how "there" and how powerful he was, his attitude, his voice, his eyes . . . At fourteen, I didn't understand the lyrics yet, but it was like an explosion of thunder in our parlor . . . I rushed to the bookstore, found a collection of his lyrics [with Italian translation] and bought my first cassette. I learned how to play the guitar. I learned "Hard Rain," it was my favorite song.[29]

Dylan came into people's lives at different stages, both of their biographies and of his own development as an artist, so he said and meant different things to each generation. This explains why there may be excellent books on Bob Dylan that devote only a couple of lines to "A Hard Rain's A-Gonna Fall" and ignore "When the Ship Comes In," and why I am writing a Dylan book in which I barely mention "Tangled Up in Blue." We are both wrong, of course. Or perhaps there are many Dylans, in different spaces and times, and he belongs entirely to none. From the beginning, he resisted labels and definitions—including his own: "It ain't me, babe" is the word.[30] The Bob Dylan in this book is only a fragment.

"I try my best to be just like I am, but everybody wants you to be just like them," he proclaims in "Maggie's Farm."[31] He had already warned us as early as the last track of my beloved *The Times They Are A-Changin'*: "I'll make my stand / And remain as I am / And bid farewell and not give a damn."[32] Actually, I didn't want Bob Dylan to be like me; if anything, sometimes and somehow, I wanted to be like him—back then, we thought a leader ought to be better than us, not just like us or worse. But that wasn't right either: "I ain't lookin' for you to feel like me, see like me, or be like me."[33] The only option, then, was to take his advice and try my best to be like I was—and like I had become, also thanks to him.

And yet: what was *he* like, Robert Zimmerman turned Bob Dylan? The most elusive word in his canon is the first person singular—what does he mean when he says "I"; is it him or just another "brilliant disguise"?[34] We early Dylan radicals caught a lot of flak when Dylan was quoted saying that those protest songs were only "a way of getting on the train of his own career,"[35] only a mask—indeed, hadn't he been wearing a mask all the while, passing himself off as a Southwestern hobo with put-on vernacular diction and a new name? "I am wearing my Bob Dylan mask," he announced as early as 1964; and, of course, he literally wore one throughout his 1975 Rolling Thunder Revue tour, lately celebrated in a Martin Scorsese film.[36]

Perhaps, then, when he rejected his early protest songs and politics, he was also wearing another of his many masks: moving on to another phase of his career did not necessarily mean reneging on all that went before.[37] Even in his restless farewell message, he had explained that "Ev'ry cause that ever I fought, I fought it full without regret or shame." I have a hard time believing that one may write "Masters of War" or "The Lonesome Death of Hattie Carroll" only as an opportunistic career move or to follow a fashion—for one thing, neither song conforms entirely to the ethics and point of view of standard early 1960s protest song. For instance, Odetta, Judy Collins, and even Pete Seeger omitted from their covers of "Masters of War" the verse in which Dylan sings to the warmongers, "I hope that you die, and your death will come soon." Peace-loving folks were not supposed to "hate." Whatever his motivation, it was Dylan's own business; a work of art, however, lives on independent of the author's intentions or explanations.[38]

As I was beginning to work on this book, nuclear missiles were flying, from Korea over Japan, and roaring out warnings across the ocean; " 'I woke up this morning in Hawaii with ten minutes to live. It was a false alarm, but a real psychic warning,' actor Jim Carrey recalled."[39] The hard rain did not fall that day, but it may be on the way. So whether Bob Dylan believed in those songs or not, the point is that *we* did. More than half a century later, "some people" are still not "allowed to be free," and many of us are still trying to believe in "causes" like opposition to war, fear of nuclear annihilation, hatred of racism, or solidarity with "the refugees on the unarmed road of flight."[40] Without regret or shame.

SHILLONG, MEGHALAYA, INDIA:
THE BOB DYLAN CAFÉ

November 2017, Shillong, India, capital of the state of Meghalaya. I am staying with a local couple, both high school teachers. My host gets up in the morning, puts Dylan records on the stereo, eats breakfast, and does not turn it off until bedtime. He is not unusual. This town, it has been said, is "obsessed with Bob Dylan."[41]

Shillong teems with music. That evening, Rida Gatphoh, a fantastic singer, and members of her group, Rida and the Musical Folks, played for me some of their songs in traditional form about contemporary themes and conflicts, the violation of nature, the rights of tribal peoples. "Our music is closely linked to nature," she explained. "Most of the songs are about the land, the trees, the wind." One of the songs they played that night was *Sur Ka Mariang* ("Tunes of Nature"): "Listen to the sound of the rain and wind, listen to the calling of the birds and insects, the animals in the forest. The sounds of nature have taught us to call out to our land with love; the stones, the trees, the rivers, the valleys remind us to call out to the creator with love to the sounds of nature."[42] She explained:

Our music is about connecting with our roots and folklore. Like Bob Dylan we write songs that are a reflection of the time we live in and capture the changes around us. Instead of being influenced by Western music and their instruments we decided to go fully acoustic using our traditional instruments to create our very own original sound. Bob Dylan has inspired us to create music with a purpose.

The next day, one hundred thousand pilgrims marched in procession, singing hymns to celebrate the Catholic feast of the Eucharist. Shillong's most important musical moment, however, is another kind of pilgrimage: a rock festival held every year on May 24, to celebrate Bob Dylan's birthday.

It began in 1972 as a get-together of friends; gradually, it became one of the top musical gatherings of Northwest India. Its founder and organizer is Lou Majaw, a musician of tribal origins, a rocker and songwriter in his own right, but, most of all, high priest of the cult of Bob Dylan. Born in 1947, he is the same age as independent India. In 1964, he recalls, he heard Bob Dylan for the first time, and was captivated "not by the voice but the words. There was such a depth to them that I couldn't think of anything else for a long time." The first time he heard "Blowin' in the Wind," at a friend's house in Kolkata, he says, "I was blown away" by the words. "That single song got me to him and changed my life."[43] It changed mine, too, and Francesco De Gregori's, and many others'. We may now say that it is sentimental, generic, boring, whatever—but no song has turned lives and changed times like "Blowin' in the Wind." A Lou Majaw performance is on YouTube; whether good or not, it doesn't matter. He drives the audience wild with a hard-rock version of "Knockin' on Heaven's Door," and invents a wacky but captivating "Mr. Tambourine Man."[44]

In Shillong, the lyrics to "Mr. Tambourine Man" are written not on "subway walls [and] tenement halls," as in Simon and Garfunkel's classic,[45] but on the sides of the soft-drink dispenser in the town's most popular venue—the famous Bob Dylan Café. Bob Dylan has never set foot in India (except, perhaps, once, to attend some friend's wedding), and there is no reason why he ought to mean anything to Shillong, or Shillong to him. I don't think he has ever heard of this place, but in this place, they have heard him and are still listening. The stairs, the walls, the ceilings of the Bob Dylan Café are covered with Dylan posters and memorabilia; blank spaces on the walls are provided for customers who wish to write their own praises of the poet. In the hall, a picture, *Dylan a la Quilled*, with Dylan's profile and the words: "All I can do is be me. Whoever that is."[46] Yes, who *is* he?

The town is holding its breath in view of the great procession; hundreds of cars are parked along the side streets, and people stand by them changing clothes and putting on makeup in public. Early in the morning, the only customer in the café is also a musician. His name is Vincent Stone, and he wants advice from Indira Chowdhury (founder of India's oral history association) and me on how to write his autobiography. "Why don't you start by recording it?" I suggest. He thinks it's a good idea, so I whip out my Zoom and, without looking at either of us, he speaks into the machine a fantastic narrative of how his father was recruited as a musician in the Indian army, was drawn into the secret service, became involved in a complicated story of espionage, guerrilla, treason, miracles in this contested and rebellious frontier enclave wedged between China, Nepal, Bhutan, Bangladesh, and Myanmar, and apparently reappeared years later in a Buddhist monastery.[47] His favorite Bob Dylan song is "Masters of War."

"I am not a fan of Bob Dylan," says Lou Majaw; he is more. "My respect for Bob Dylan is as a lyricist. Not as a man or a star. I am neither besotted with his looks nor bedazzled by his charisma. I celebrate the strength of his writing, the depth of his lyrics." His most acclaimed Dylan performance is "Rainy Day Women #12 & 35." Across the street from the Bob Dylan Café, in the corner of a huge no-parking graffiti, someone stenciled Bob Dylan's curly profile, and the song's immortal words: "Everybody must get stoned." Even in Shillong, someone is still "draw[ing] conclusions on the walls."[48]

STOCKHOLM, SWEDEN:
BRINGING IT ALL BACK HOME

Then, one day Bob Dylan told me, "Most like you go your way and I'll go mine,"[49] and I took him literally. We traveled together as far as *Blonde on Blonde* and *John Wesley Harding*, past his famous electric turn, then I took one road and he another (he is probably still wondering how many roads he must go down before he knows who he is). The things that he was looking for were not the ones I sought, and vice versa. Some felt betrayed;

I didn't. Bob Dylan is not the only person who lived through a youthful season of political passion and then changed, became someone else, grew up, grew younger ("I was so much older then . . .") and kept looking, for an identity, for other revolutions, for success, for all these things together and others and more. I still feel for him, I keep in touch, but I don't encounter him as often as I used to. I relate to his later work somewhat like he relates to the work of other poets—Blake, Rilke, Dante. "I understand what's there, it's just that the connection sometimes does not connect." My fault, I guess.[50]

So, I never thought I would again write about Bob Dylan, until he was awarded the Nobel Prize and I was forcibly dragged into it by the insistence of my Italian publisher, Carmine Donzelli. There is something uncannily right in the fact that Bob Dylan's name was announced on the same day as the passing of another controversial laureate, Dario Fo. Both Dylan and Fo are untypical laureates in the lineage of an often-stiff highbrow institution. Both have been labeled as intruders in the precinct of "literature," yet literature owes a great deal to both of them. By rooting their creativity in the realm of oral, popular folk cultures, they have changed our perception of language and reminded us of how indissolubly linked poetry is with sound, voice, body, improvisation, performance, and orality. In Dario Fo's "Mistero Buffo" and "The Accidental Death of an Anarchist," in Bob Dylan's "A Hard Rain's A-Gonna Fall" or "The Lonesome Death of Hattie Carroll"—and in the oral histories of another atypical Nobel laureate, Svetlana Alexievich—the oral voices of street artists, vagrants, and mountebanks from the Italian countryside; of

Mississippi Delta field hands and Depression hobos; of Chernobyl survivors and Afghanistan veterans move from the margin to the center of culture and become the new languages of our time. Alessandro Carrera claims that Dylan's later work is the greatest modernist poem in American literature. He is probably right. As for me, if I believed in the Nobel Prize at all, I think he might deserve it on the strength of "A Hard Rain's A-Gonna Fall" alone. Throughout his work, and signally in this masterpiece, Bob Dylan has rooted the languages of the present and the future on the heritage of a centuries-old oral tradition, thus changing the imagination and the life of three generations and more. In Dario Fo's work, the Nobel Prize recognized the deep seriousness of humor and satire. In Dylan's, it recognized a whole world of long-ignored and discounted popular arts. The margin seizes the center. In a way, this is a political achievement, too.

Which is why, fortunately, not everyone agrees. Friends and comrades I respect and admire were offended; even the radical paper for which I usually write, echoed by most other media, editorialized that Dylan's Nobel Prize was a "conformist" choice, dictated by market and commercial considerations. The fact is, however, that the Nobel Prize is inherently conformist: it functions as a consecration, a call for unanimity and celebration that creates conformity, even where it did not exist before. I wonder whether, had the award been granted to perennial candidate Philip Roth, or my favorite Don DeLillo—let alone Jonathan Franzen—our critics would have hailed it as a bold and daring act of nonconformity. If anything, instead, the furor and dissent over Bob Dylan suggest that this time it was a more surprising and unpredictable choice than most.

Of course, one may legitimately claim that Dylan did not deserve it because he is not a great artist. In this case, right or wrong, we would only be doing our job as critics. But the claim that he should not have been recognized because his work is not literature is more problematic. In my academic career, I have taught plenty of literature classes that included Bob Dylan and Robert Johnson, the blues and the popular ballad, Woody Guthrie and Bruce Springsteen, and though I began when no one had heard of "cultural studies," I don't think I was alone. The question, then, is not the quality of Dylan's art, but what kind of art it is; whether, in the third millennium, we still think of literature in the same terms as the late-nineteenth-century founders of the Nobel Prize.

For at least a century and a half, since the advent of new "technologies of the word"[51]—cinema, radio, sound recording—the printed word is no longer the only medium to which we entrust the exploration of language, the invention of visions, the telling of stories; that is, the essential functions of what we call literature. On the other hand, in centuries past and still today, all over the world, orality and song have been and are the medium through which human beings have told and sung their stories and poems. If there is one thing we can say about Bob Dylan—and this is what the pages that follow will be about—it is that he has bridged different realms of language and imagination, sustaining a modernist sensibility and a technological imagination on the basis of centuries of oral cultures.

One day in the mid-seventies, Agostino Lombardo, the dean of my department of English and American Studies, got a phone call from the Canadian embassy. A young Canadian poet was coming to Rome, and they wondered whether we could invite him to speak to our students. Lombardo had never heard of him, but he was trying to promote Canadian studies anyway, so he agreed. To his surprise, on the appointed day, hundreds of avidly expectant students were climbing all over the walls of the main conference hall. Then the poet stepped on the stage, picked up a guitar and started: "Suzanne takes you down to her place near the river. . . ." His name was Leonard Cohen— another "half breed" artist, here, there, and nowhere. In another song, "A Singer Must Die," accused of betraying poetry by contaminating it with music, the singer accepts the tribunal's death sentence with humble pride: "I thank you, I thank you for doing your duty, you keepers of truth, you guardians of beauty; your vision is right, my vision is wrong, I'm sorry for smudging the air with my song."[52]

Dylan, too, smudged our air with his unbearable voice. Yes, he does deserve the prize, some critics objected, but it should have been for music, not poetry. I can imagine the protest of "real" musicians—"do you call this 'music'? he's just a pop singer. . . ." And so on. The point, however, is that in order to recognize artists like Bob Dylan, we ought not so much add new categories (there is no Nobel Prize for music anyway), but rather rethink the categories that we have, redefine their shape and boundaries, and ultimately question the value of categorizing and parsing knowledge and art, history, and memory into rigidly separate fields. Artists like Dylan do not fit categories, but overstep them, mix them, confound them, take us along the path of doubt and searching—which, after all, is what art and literature are for. Bob Dylan does not belong in literature, because we cannot lock him inside it. We ought to thank him for challenging us to rethink Jean Paul Sartre's question—*qu'est-ce que la littérature?*—and leaving the answer to blow in the wind.

Chapter One

SONGS OF INNOCENCE AND EXPERIENCE

POISON AND RAIN

Bob Dylan wrote "A Hard Rain's A-Gonna Fall" in New York in the summer of 1962, between the building of the Berlin wall and the Cuban missile crisis.

> Oh, where have you been, my blue-eyed son
> Where have you been, my darling young one?
> I've stumbled on the side of twelve misty mountains
> I've walked and I've crawled over six crooked
>   highways . . .

In 1629, a collection of songs published in Verona, Italy, by an obscure writer known as Camillo il Bianchino, quoted the first lines of a song: "Dov'andastu iersera figliuol mio ricco, savio e gentile? Dov'andastu iersera?"("Where have you been last night, my rich, wise and gentle son? / Where did you go last night?")[1] Two and a half centuries later, in the village of Loveno, near Como, in Lombardy, two young women sang:

Dove si stà iersira, figliol mio caro fiorito e gentil
Dove si stà iersira?
So sta' da la mia dama, signora mama mio core sta mal
So sta' da la mia dama, ahimé, ch'io moro ahimé.[2]
(Where have you been last night, my dear, flowery and
gentle son?
Where have you been last night?
I went to see my lady,
I went to see my lady, alas, I'm dying, alas.)

Bob Dylan first performed "A Hard Rain's A-Gonna Fall" in public on September 22, 1962, in a folk song hootenanny organized by Pete Seeger at Carnegie Hall. The song was published for the first time in the folk-song magazine *Sing Out!* in December 1962; Bob Dylan recorded it in New York's Studio A on December 6, 1962, and it was included in his first album of original songs, *The Freewheelin' Bob Dylan*, issued on May 27, 1963.[3]

In 1701, in Edinburgh, Scotland, someone transcribed the words of a ballad in a domestic notebook. It went like this:

O where ha you been, Lord Randal, my son?
And where ha you been, my handsome young one?
I hae been at the greenwood; mother, mak my bed soon
For I'm wearied wi hunting, and I fan would lie doon.

A century and a half later, Harvard professor Francis J. Child saw the notebook, and included the song as "Lord Randal" as number 12 of his canonic *The English and Scottish Popular Ballads*, published in 1882–1888.[4] Child notes that although the ballad exists in different versions throughout Europe, from Sweden to Catalonia, the closest textual affinity exists between the Italian and the British variants. "Lord Randal," in fact, is most popular in the Scottish and Northern Irish area, from Aberdeen to Belfast. Jeannie Robertson, the great traveler singer from Aberdeen, sang it as "Lord Donald, My Son":

> Whaur hae ye been all the day, Lord Donald my son
> Whaur hae ye been all the day, my jolly young man?
> Awa' courtin', mither, mak' my bed soon
> For I am sick at the hairt and I fain would lie doon.[5]

At more or less the same time as Child, the Italian diplomat and scholar Costantino Nigra included the Italian version of the ballad as number 26 in his canonic *Canti popolari del Piemonte* (Folk songs of Piedmont), with the title "Il testamento dell'avvelenato" (The poisoned man's testament). While Nigra only mentions Northern Italian variants, the song has been popular all over Italy. Gianni Bosio and Clara Longhini recorded it as far South as Otranto, Puglia, in 1968;[6] the last time I heard it in the field, it was performed by a Calabrian migrant named Carmela Luci in Casalotti, a working-class neighborhood of Rome, in 1973. She recalled that the vineyard owners in her home village required their farm hands to sing it while working, to make sure they weren't using their mouths to eat the grapes. She skipped the first verse and began:

> Arsira jì a la zita, mamma lu core mi sento ca mor
> Arsira jì a la zita, ahimé ch'io morerò.[7]
> (Last night I went to see my lady, mother I'm sick to the heart
> I went to see my lady, alas, I'm going to die.)

Young Bob Dylan might have heard "Lord Randal" from a 1954 Harry Belafonte 45 rpm record (of which I also owned a copy).[8] He probably also heard it around Greenwich Village from Jean Ritchie, who had learned it from her coal-mining family in Viper, Kentucky:

> Oh Where have you been, Lord Randal my son?
> Oh Where have you been, my handsome young one?
> I've been to the wildwood, mother make my bed soon
> I'm weary with hunting and I fain would lie down.[9]

Bob Dylan renewed the copyright for "A Hard Rain's A-Gonna Fall" in 1991. Meanwhile, "Il testamento dell'avvelenato" safely crossed the gates of the third millennium. In 2005, Giovanna Nobili, a farm hand and former rice field worker, sang it in Dorno, near Pavia, Lombardy:

> Si ch't'è mangià iarsira figlio mio Enrico
> Si ch't'è mangià iarsira o cavaliere gentile.[10]
> (What did you have for dinner last night, Henry my son
> What did you have for dinner my gentle knight?)

In 2016, Bob Dylan was awarded the Nobel Prize for literature. At the award ceremony in Stockholm, in his absence, Patti Smith chose to sing, out of his hundreds of songs, "A Hard Rain's A-Gonna Fall."[11]

LINKS IN THE CHAIN

As Patti Smith's choice indicates, "A Hard Rain's A-Gonna Fall" is one of the most important, if not *the* most important song in the Nobel Prize winner's canon, thus perhaps in the whole canon of twentieth century poetry. "Lord Randal" / "Il testamento dell'avvelenato" is in turn one of the most important creations of European and American folk cultures of the last five hundred years.

All Bob Dylan scholars and critics recognize the connection between the incipit of "A Hard Rain's A-Gonna Fall" and "Lord Randal," yet, in most cases, they go no further. Alessandro Carrera, for instance, comments that the original ballad "has evidently very little to do with what Bob Dylan made of it."[12] This, however, depends on the fact that most Dylan critics and fans only become aware of "Lord Randal" as a marginal philological or biographical detail of Dylan's opus, rather than as a complex and important cultural text in its own right.

In this book, I will travel in the opposite direction. After all, I had heard "Lord Randal," in that Harry Belafonte record, five or six years before I first heard "Hard Rain" (I discovered "Il testamento dell'avvelenato" from Sandra Mantovani's 1963 recording at roughly the same time I first discovered "Hard Rain"). Thus,

I learned, studied, and taught "Lord Randal" and "Il testamento dell'avvelenato" for what they are in and of themselves, not as a footnote to something else; at the same time, the first time I presented at a Rome University seminar on modern American poetry, I discussed "A Hard Rain's A-Gonna Fall" in its own right, not as a late variant of "Lord Randal." After all, the ballad had been around for at least four centuries by the time Bob Dylan heard it, and it may still be around somewhere in Europe or America. On the other hand, who knows whether four hundred years from now someone will be listening to Bob Dylan— though the quick pace of history, the weakening of memory, and the changes in technology make it problematic. As for me, I loved both "A Hard Rain's A-Gonna Fall" and "Lord Randal" completely and equally, and I know that, if we recognize their dialogue between equals, the echoes and dissonances between them can help us reach a more complex understanding and a deeper enjoyment of both.[13]

Bob Dylan's relationship with the oral tradition of the ballad or the blues is much deeper than mere covers, quotes, or echoes of lines or tunes. Many years ago, after listening to some of my field recordings of Lazio folk songs, Giovanna Marini— Italy's greatest folk singer and composer—told me, "This is my placenta." In different forms and ways, this is what folk music—ballads, blues, Woody Guthrie, Hank Williams, Charlie Patton—is for Bob Dylan: flesh and blood of his own creativity, a learned tongue in which he invents new words that are only his own. The relationship between "Blowin' in the Wind" and "No More Auction Block for Me," or between "I Pity the Poor Immigrant" and "Tramps and Hawkers," is like the one between Woody Guthrie's "So Long It's Been Good to Know You" and "The Ballad of Billy The Kid," or Giovanna Marini's "Lamento per la morte di Pasolini" and the Abruzzi folk litany "Orazione di San Donato";[14] not an old tune reused as a vehicle for new words, but a musical memory so deeply internalized that it can be freely used and changed, in the creative moment, perhaps without even being aware of it.[15]

Some, of course, see this relationship as mere theft. In his postmodern African American epic, *Mumbo Jumbo* (1972), Ishmael Reed invents a parable in which Moses goes down to Ethiopia, learns from Jethro the deep secrets of African culture, and uses them to rise in Pharaoh's court. The allusion to Bob Dylan and his harmonica is transparent:

> That night Jethro took out his instrument that must have had about 25 strings. He then put some kind of early styled harmonica in his mouth. And with his feet he beat on some kind of tinny thing. Then he started twanging on that many-stringed monstrosity and zipping his fingers up and down that thing and making that thing cry. . . . Moses asked Jethro if he would mind if he wrote all of this down. . . . Well when Moses had learned all of Jethro's songs and had made Jethro create upon these strange instruments he played, Moses packed his papyri instruments and was bidding Jethro goodbye. He said he would play his songs in the temples and while he played them he would always have a kind place in his heart for Jethro.[16]

Bob Dylan's ironic response is his 2001 album *"Love and Theft."* As we know, Dylan's title quotes (literally: the quotation marks are his) Eric Lott's innovative study of the minstrel show tradition, *Love and Theft: Blackface Minstrelsy and the American Working Class* (1993).[17] Lott shows in that book that minstrel show is not just a theft and parody of Black culture, but also the expression of a repressed desire that sustains all of American popular culture. By this reference, Dylan recognizes his own appropriation of Black culture—indeed, as the album's track list shows, of all folk culture—as the nutriment of his own creative artistic imagination.

A key passage in this process is Bob Dylan's so-called rebirth in the 1990s. As Sean Wilentz writes, "Now that Dylan was feeling as if his creativity, if not exactly shut off like a faucet, had severely slowed . . . he returned to his musical roots, continuing to add traditional material to his concerts and listening to fresh collections of blues, mountain songs, contemporary folk music, and more."[18] It is alright to discuss Dylan's "roots," but only if we think of them not as a fixed past buried under the earth, but as an active source of new life—placenta, indeed. "If you can sing those [folk] songs," Dylan explains, "if you can understand those songs and can perform them well, there's nowhere you *can't* go."[19] We would not have *Time Out of Mind*, "*Love and Theft*," *Modern Times*, or *Tempest* without *Good as I Been to You* and *World Gone Wrong* immediately before them. These albums were Bob Dylan's re-immersion in the poetic and musical universe of folk music, a creative ground that renewed his power and sent him on toward new territories. As Greil Marcus noted, "the old songs that sprung to such cryptic life on *Good as I Been to You* and *World Gone Wrong* took a new form in 1997 with *Time Out of Mind*."[20] This is what Giovanna Marini meant that day: without the nutriment of the oral tradition, neither she nor Bob Dylan could have invented the new forms of expression that make them special.

In the 1960s, Pete Seeger used to write a column, "The Folk Process" in *Sing Out!* It was about how songs change and evolve as they pass from mouth to mouth, adapting to different functions and contexts, and thus remain timely and alive. Bob Dylan is part of this process, but he also takes a step forward and carries the "folk process" to a new level. If every singer is, in Pete Seeger's words, "a link in the chain,"[21] then Bob Dylan is a link between many chains, a link that connects and renews many different traditions and languages, giving them new power and keeping them alive.

Another American bard, Walt Whitman, proclaimed:

> Through me many long dumb voices,
> Voices of the interminable generations of prisoners and
>   slaves
>
> . . .
>
> Through me forbidden voices,
> Voices of sexes and lusts, voices veil'd and I remove the
>   veil,
> Voices indecent by me clarified and transfigur'd.[22]

In the case of Bob Dylan, these words are literally true—with a caveat. Bob Dylan is a great voice of modernity, but he would not be if his voice didn't resonate with the "transfigur'd," forbidden, and indecent voices of times past. Whitman, however, seems to suggest that these voices can only be heard through his own; if he had not removed "the veil," they would remain forever "dumb" and un-clarified. Yet, this is not true. Bob Dylan, like many others, has helped, as they say, "give voice" to prisoners, slaves, and other generations of oppressed, forgotten, marginalized folk. These people, however, were not "dumb" at all; they already had a voice of their own. They spoke, they sang, and it is by listening to their voices that Bob Dylan has received his own. Without "Lord Randal," there would be no "A Hard Rain's A-Gonna Fall," at least not as we know it now.

"A Hard Rain's A-Gonna Fall" is one of those links between chains. It thrives on the historical depths incorporated in the ancient ballad, projects it toward a modern and postmodern imagination, and illuminates both. It springs out of a magical moment in which Bob Dylan was between worlds and in touch with both, still part of the folk music revival but ready to leave it for shores unknown. Where has he been, our blue-eyed brother and son?

THE WILDWOOD AND THE HOME

Rolling Stone defines "A Hard Rain's A-Gonna Fall" as "The greatest protest song by the greatest protest songwriter of his time: a seven-minute epic that warns against a coming apocalypse while cataloging horrific visions."[23] It is more than a "protest song," but for the moment let us leave it as that. What I would like to do instead is say a few things about how we define "Lord Randal."

"Il testamento dell'avvelenato" / "Lord Randal" is a ballad (I will use "Lord Randal" to refer to the whole of its Italian, British, and American variants). The tersest definition of *ballad* is "a folk-song that tells a story":[24] a narrative song transmitted mainly through the oral tradition and known mainly among the non-hegemonic, popular classes.[25] If "Lord Randal" is a song that tells a story, then, what story does it tell?

Like "Hard Rain," "Lord Randal" is a dialogue between a mother and a son. The young man has gone out of the house, to hunt and to visit his "true love." He comes home and asks his mother to make his bed because he is ill and feels that he is dying. His mother asks what he had for dinner, who served it, and how. In most cases, it is fried eels or fried fish—as Carmela Luci sang—"in a new skillet" and served with new silver. In many versions, such as Ewan MacColl's, he feeds half of it to his dogs, and "they swelled and they died."[26] She tells him that he has been poisoned and asks him to make his will. I will discuss the form and contents of the will later. At this point, however, the question is: why did the young man's "true love" poison him? And what kind of mother is this who, as her son is dying, asks him about the contents of his will?

This question would make sense if "Lord Randal" were a novel, a short story, a film—genres with realistic characters who require motivations and some kind of psychological consistency. The ballad, however, is not about this. The passage of time and the myriad voices and memories that have reshaped it as they passed it on have honed and polished it until only the essentials remain. This is, in fact, the function of memory, especially, though not only, in oral cultures; not a detailed dia-chronic record of people and events, but a synchronic conden-sation of their meaning. Thus, the ballad is not about lifelike characters, but about abstract archetypes and functions that stage dramatic and inextricable moral, social, and historical conflicts and contradictions. The young man is caught in the eternal conflict between the known (the home, the bed) and the unknown (the "wildwood," the hunting grounds), the famil-iar (the mother) and the new (the lover), the tensions between safety and adventure, continuity and change, "descent" and "consent."[27] Like all tragic heroes, he belongs to both worlds; he embodies continuity because he is a son, and change because he is young. There is more to this story, but once again for now we will leave it at that.

As already noted, "Hard Rain" and "Lord Randal" share the same structure: a dialogue between a mother and a son. The mother is mentioned explicitly in the ballad ("Mother, make my bed soon . . ."), while in Dylan's song it is suggested implic-itly both by the relationship with the ballad ("my darling young one" echoes the mother's words in the first lines of the ballad) and by the association between mother and home. Only a few commentators have suggested that the blue-eyed son may be speaking to his father,[28] and the absence of the father in both songs in fact makes more sense. In the ballad, the father is either absent or powerless. The hero must have a mother to return to and to make his bed, but he must also be the head of the family in order to be entitled to make a will. The mother stands for the presence of the past, but the hero's will projects the story toward the future. In "Hard Rain," the absence of the father as an authority figure responds to the generational themes of the movements of the 1960s, when Bob Dylan was urging fathers and mothers to get out of the way if they couldn't lend a hand and denouncing those fathers who, like Abraham's God, invite their believers to "kill me a son," in the forests of Vietnam.[29] Like all young rebels, Dylan's blue-eyed son has no burden of history on his shoulders, as if the world began with him and he was the first to discover its horrors.

THE TRANSPARENT EYEBALL

"Hard Rain," then, uses the basic story and structure of "Lord Randal" to reset the story to a different context and time and create new meaning. In this process, Bob Dylan introduces a detail of his own that is not found in any version or variant of the ballad: Lord Randal is "bonnie" in Scotland, "handsome" in Kentucky and North Carolina, always "gentle" and often "flowery" in Italy. But only in Bob Dylan is he ever "blue-eyed."

The blue-eyed son has the clear, limpid eyes of innocence; he does no evil, and indeed, he does not even know that there is such a thing as evil in the world. He is Adam before the fall, an errant knight in shining armor.[30] The loss of innocence as the price for adult experience is a classic theme in American literature; the naïve adolescent hero goes out into the world, like Huckleberry Finn down the Mississippi, and is initiated to the knowledge and the presence of evil and death.[31]

"I've been *out* in front of a dozen dead oceans"; the danger is *out there*, in the "wildwood," in the dead oceans, the misty mountains, the depths of the grave. Both "Lord Randal" and "Hard Rain" are about a young man, a son, who leaves home, walks and crawls through dangerous unknown lands and deadly encounters, discovers evil, violence, betrayal, and death, and comes home to tell the tale and prepare to die. "Lord Randal" remains innocent unto the end; he doesn't even realize that it was his "true love" who poisoned him until his mother tells him. In his initiation journey, Dylan's blue-eyed son meets icons of innocence violated: a newborn baby surrounded by wolves, young children wielding guns and sharp swords, a child near a dead pony, and the place where the idyllic "home in the valley" meets, or becomes, the gothic "damp dirty prison." "We never thought we could ever get old," he sang in "Bob Dylan's Dream." Innocents are "forever young," they don't believe in their own death.[32] But the only way we can be forever young is to "die before we get old," as the Who taught us, and this is in fact the fate of the hero at the end of "Hard Rain." In those rooms where he spent his adolescent evenings with the friends of his youth, "the thought never hit / That the one road we traveled would ever shatter or split." The future was a straight and open road that they would travel in harmony without risk of violence, conflict, or doubt. Yet as the blue-eyed son leaves home, he meets darkness, confusion, and deception; the roads are many (at least six) and they are "crooked," not just geometrically, but morally, they are dishonest.

In a famous passage, Ralph Waldo Emerson wrote:

In the woods, is perpetual youth. . . There I feel that nothing can befall me in life—no disgrace, no calamity, leaving me my eyes, which nature cannot repair. Standing on the bare ground—my head bathed by the blithe air, and uplifted into infinite space—all mean egotism vanishes. I become a transparent eye-ball; I am nothing; I see all; the currents of the Universal Being circulate through me; I am part or particle of God.[33]

The clear pupil of the blue-eyed son is also transparent, but only in one direction: it reveals the purity of his soul inside, but there is no transparence in nature outside: the mountains are misty, the oceans are dead, the forests sad. No mystic currents flow between God, Nature, and Soul. Dylan's forest is less like Emerson's benevolent woods than the "wildwood" where Lord Randal meets his fate, or the wilderness that his Puritan ancestors knew to be filled with unknown dangers and evil presences—like the "dark, demonic woods" out of which Dylan himself says he has come.[34] About the same time as Emerson found vision and illumination in the woods, Nathaniel Hawthorne reminded his contemporaries that "the founders of a new colony, whatever Utopia of human virtue and happiness they might originally project, have invariably recognized it among their earliest practical necessities to allot a portion of the virgin soil as a cemetery, and another portion as the site of a prison."[35] The mouth of a graveyard is where the blue-eyed hero steps at the beginning of his journey; and the "damp dirty prison" is what he will meet in the end.

THE BLUEST EYE

I started work on this book after a year spent editing an Italian-language critical edition of the selected novels of Toni Morrison. Thus, I inevitably connected Dylan's blue-eyed son with the title of Morrison's first novel. *The Bluest Eye* is the story of an African American child, Pecola Breedlove, who is obsessed with the dream of having blue eyes, like the child actors she sees in the movies and in ads. Indeed, as a rule, Black people do not have blues eyes. Which is why, in their rendering of "Hard Rain," the Black gospel group Staple Singers change it to "my wondering son," and Jimmy Cliff's reggae version is not about a blue-eyed son but a "brown-eyed" one.[36]

This difference is less about skin color than about the expectations, about the sense of one's standing in the world that it entails. In this sense, there is an uncanny reverberation between "Hard Rain" and Bruce Springsteen's "Born in the U.S.A."; being born (white) in the United States carries a promise, a sense of entitlement, that is brutally betrayed when you leave home to discover death and treason in the "sad forests" of Vietnam and return home to find yourself stranded, burning down the road by the hellish fires of the refinery.

Black children and mothers do not need journeys into the unknown in order to discover what awaits them in the wilderness outside. In Bruce Springsteen's "Black Cowboys," little Rainey Williams makes his way to the playground through spaces as filled with danger and death at those crossed by Dylan's hero: "Names and photos of the young black faces

/ Whose death and blood consecrated these places." His mother does not ask him who he met, what he saw, what he heard—she knows very well what those streets are like. She just wants him to come home from school and stay inside—perhaps, like Lord Randal's mother, to make his bed. Unlike the mother in Dylan's song, Black children's parents speak to them *before* they leave home. New York City mayor Bill DeBlasio, whose son is Black, explained, "[My wife] Chirlane and I have had to talk to [our son] Dante for years, about the dangers he may face. . . . we've had to literally train him, as families have all over this city for decades, in how to take special care in any encounter he has with the police officers who are there to protect him."[37] Springsteen again speaks to this in "American Skin":

> On these streets, Charles
> You've got to understand the rules
> If an officer stops you, promise me you'll always be polite
> And that you'll never ever run away
> Promise Mama you'll keep your hands in sight.[38]

Only those who believe in innocence—their own and of others—only those who leave home believing that they have rights and are safe, can be shocked at the unexpected discovery of violence and evil. I am reminded of the stories told by student activists of the sixties about their surprise at discovering that the police didn't beat only the workers but attacked them, too.[39] "You know, the big demonstrations were those of the workers, not us students, so we were totally naïve. At first the march was playful, a holiday, a game. Then it turned out that it was no game at all. They gave us a real serious drubbing. It was relatively tough."[40] Or the tragic events, the killing of a young man, the police riots at the 2001 G8 summit in Genoa, when the "gentle" and "flowery" young people of the third millennium lost their "innocence" in a bloody confrontation with the violence of the state. "We lost our virginity. A very naïve movement was suddenly confronted with the hardness of reality, with the actuality of violent conflict."[41]

> We were out in the street, dancing, playing living theater and all. They come at us from behind . . . And I couldn't understand what was going on . . . I mean, shedding all at once the belief of twenty-one years that the police is there to protect you . . . I was wondering—why are they attacking us? . . . Here I am, dancing, with sunflowers in my hair, and you beat me up? Why?[42]

Of course, Bob Dylan wasn't thinking of Genoa 2001 when he wrote "Hard Rain" forty years earlier. But he possessed the vision that can turn a historical moment into a timeless archetype—which is, in the end, the "inner substance" that makes a song a folk song and keeps it alive in history.[43] Bob Dylan can reap this wonder without even having to wait for the years to pass. He hardly ever writes topical songs, and when he does, they are not his best; but out of historic events—the murder of Medgar Evers, the lonesome death of Hattie Carroll, the atomic nightmare of the fifties and sixties—he distills warnings for all time. His songs never lose touch with immediate events, but also reach for the deep historical forces that shape them and consign the news of the day to the long duration of archetype or myth, so that the story of the present foreshadows those of the future. The "guns and sharp swords in the hands of young children" announce the child soldiers of the civil war in Sierra Leone, wielding machine guns and machetes at the dawn of the third millennium. We have all seen "a white man who walked a black dog" in the images from Abu Ghraib. The "one hundred drummers whose hands were a-blazin' " are also the threatening police squadrons that marched in formation in Genoa, beating rhythmically with their clubs on their plastic shields, the dark visors of their helmets lowered to cover their eyes because, as we know, "the executioner's face is always well hidden."

NO DIRECTION HOME: A DIGRESSION

We talk to Noemi . . . in August 2017, in her lawyer's satellite office. Noemi has a green card. She is wearing a red blouse with her hair pulled back, accentuating her large brown eyes.[44]

I was halfway through the writing of this book when another epiphany hit me as I looked at a picture of African migrants, mostly from the former Italian colony of Eritrea, stranded on the boulders on the beach of Ventimiglia, trying in vain to cross the French-Italian border. For the last ten years I had been working on a project on the oral history and music of immigrants in Italy. As I looked at the picture, it struck me that they, too, didn't have blue eyes.[45] Yet, I thought, thanks to the Staple Singers and Jimmy Cliff, "Hard Rain" may also be about them.

Migrants from the South of the world, exiles, "refugees on the unarmed road of flight," do not have the right color of eyes and skin. As they try to cross into the United States and Europe, over multiple borders and across the sea, these brown-eyed wandering daughters and sons literally walk and crawl over crooked highways, step through misty mountains and sad forests, stand in front of deadly oceans, meet police with bleeding hammers or white men walking black dogs,[46] whisper and speak unheeded with broken tongues, and end up in damp dirty prisons—like brown-eyed Noemi Tun, from Guatemala, who was sixteen when she crossed into the United States:

> The *coyotes* abandoned us in the desert somewhere near the US-Mexico border. After two days of walking without food or water, we heard the engines of an airplane nearby in the middle of the night. . . . When the agents came, I actually felt happy because I didn't want to suffer more after being for lost two days and two nights without water. . . .
>
> So they brought us to a *hielera* in McAllen, Texas. . . . There were around ten kids in the *hielera*, a lot of people packed into this small room. They were all twelve, thirteen, fourteen years old, all girls more or less the same age as us. My sister and I didn't know any of the other people. Everyone was crying because they had told all of us that we would be deported to our countries. They gave us a thin mattress to lie on but no blanket. The floor was cement and cold. They

kept the lights on the whole time. At one point, they tossed some cookies and orange juice into the room.[47]

The African migrants had come over the sea on boats, rafts, and dinghies, undocumented, bearing expectations and hopes,[48] and had stood on the ocean until thousands started sinking. ("From January to June 2021, it was estimated that 827 migrants died while crossings the Mediterranean Sea. In 2020, the number of deaths amounted to 1.4 thousand. However, an accurate account of deaths in the Mediterranean Sea cannot be ascertained. Between 2014 and 2018, for instance, about 12 thousand people who drowned were never found.")[49] One hundred thirty sank in the Mediterranean on April 27, 2021, as I was revising this book. Three hundred drowned in view of the Italian island of Lampedusa, October 3, 2013, a date since celebrated each year as the day of memory of migration. Rashid, twenty-one years old, from the former Italian colony of Somalia, was on that boat:

The boat sails at night, travels through the morning, but when the sun is high the problems begin, the boat stops. There are many people inside, Christians, Muslims, but we all pray. We pray and cry. Those below want to come up, they're afraid if the boat breaks and the water comes in they are stuck in there. Those outside are against it, but they scream, there are problems . . . I can do nothing, I just wait. But I realize that the engine is broken, there's a problem. The boat is broken, the engine broken, no gasoline, gasoline all around the boat, my head is reeling because there's no air. We are stuck in the middle of the sea. Then those on top see a big ship in the distance, and they all stand up to call the big ship and the boat turns over. I don't know when the water breaks in, some swim, some don't. I don't know how I get out. I can only swim a little. The boat is half sunk, all are clinging to it, some die, we've been in the water three hours, those who don't know how to swim die . . . I find a dead person that is floating, I cling to him so I don't sink, don't die. So many died.[50]

"When I reach Italy, after all this time," says Rashid, "I am no longer afraid to die." And yet, how does it feel to be without a home, like a complete unknown, a "rank stranger" in an alien land?[51] Another young Somali migrant, Geedi Yusuf, put it in a song: "I'm a foreigner, I'm a stranger, I'm a guest in Italy / I run, run to school, to learn Italian / I am African, I am running from the beasts who bear arms / We're not Africans, we're not Europeans, what are we all?"[52] I still have his picture in my phone, and his eyes are brown. He explained:

When I arrived here I didn't understand the language and I kept hearing this word, *stanier, stranier* [stranger, foreigner], and I didn't know what it means and what the people who addressed me by this word meant, I was wondering what it meant, it must be an insult, it must mean stupid, something like that. [And then] I understood that it was a word that was used for refugees, for people who came from outside, to designate the people who were not part of this country, of this place. In fact in the first verse I also say *ospite* [guest], I learned this word when I received my *permesso di soggiorno* [temporary residence permit]. *Permesso di* soggiorno—permit to remain for *giorni* [days]. Somalis have no recognized passport, we were asked to pay to have a *titolo di viaggio* [travel permit], to move . . . These three things—the word *straniero*, the *permesso di soggiorno*, the *titolo di viaggio* made me understand that I have no law that makes me an equal here, but I am only a guest.

The subversive core of Geedi's song is the word *osbitaan*, a migrant's (mis)pronunciation of *ospite*, the Italian word that means both "host" and "guest." *Ospite* is one of the hypocritical words that allow native Italians to feel good about ourselves because we as *hosts* allow these people to come into *our* country as *guests*. As a young Somali migrant explained, "A newborn baby needs time, needs food, needs care, needs education." Like newborn babies with wolves all around them, "we have no parents, we are guests and this country doesn't help us, either economically or psychologically."[53] As Geedi explains, a guest can only stay "for days"; you will never be allowed to call this country your home, you are only welcome here temporarily, as a sojourner (*soggiorno*), like a rolling stone with only one right: to keep moving, with no direction home.

Not even that. The migrants massed on the border at Ventimiglia were indeed "condemned to drift" and yet "kept from drifting."[54] They wanted to keep moving, across one more border, but the European union has abolished borders only for those with the right skin color.[55] I can cross into France anytime I want; they were bound to stay, not as guests but as captives, in a country that didn't want them. On the boulders by the beach, "souls trapped between Italy and France" (as another migrant poet describes them), they improvised a call-and-response song with makeshift percussions, in true African style, made only of one line: "We are not / Going back." Refugees on the unarmed road of flight, they keep on knocking on heaven's doors, trying to get to heaven before they close the door.[56]

Chapter Two

THE TEXT AND THE VOICE

TIME

In a seminal 1930 essay, Roman Jakobson and Petr Bogatyrev described folklore as a "special form of creation"; a song or a tale only becomes a *folk* song or a *folk* tale when they are shared, adopted, filtered, and changed by the "consent of a community." A folk song gains new life and energy each time someone sings it, and it dies when no one deems it worth singing or remembering.[1] Therefore, a folk song has no original or authentic text or tune. It exists only as the whole of its existing or possible variants and versions. A ballad is all its history and prehistory (according to Betsy Miller, who taught it to her son Ewan Mac-Coll, "Lord Randal" is a true story that happened in Scotland "God knows when"),[2] its past and its future. "Il testamento dell'avvelenato" as sung by Giovanna Nobili in 2005 is as original and authentic as whatever version Bianchino might have heard in 1629. What counts is less the song's origin and antiquity than its persistence and presence.

Jakobson and Bogatyrev, however, insist on the folk process as a process of transformation ("filter"); oral cultures alter as they preserve—indeed, we might say that they alter in order to preserve, so that older cultural "texts" remain viable as times and contexts change. As we know, no one tells one's life story exactly the same way in different contexts, at different times, to different listeners;[3] likewise, no one can sing a song exactly as they heard it or sing it twice in the same manner. All singers must retrieve the song from the depths of memory and reinvent it so that it may respond to the performers' own sense of their historical persona at the same time as it makes sense to a given audience at a given place and time.[4]

Thus, each new performance is a new interpretation, both in the artistic and in the hermeneutical sense. As Dennis Tedlock pointed out, in oral performance we are getting both the text and the criticism at the same time and from the same person.[5] The ballad is always itself but never the same: far from being timeless, it only lives in time and changes with history. It can branch out and become unrecognizable; "Il testamento dell'avvelenato" can evolve into a World War I soldier song, and "Lord Randal" can turn into "Where have you been, Billy Boy, Billy Boy / Where have you been all the day, charming Billy?"[6]

Bob Dylan's "A Hard Rain's A-Gonna Fall," on the other hand, does exist in an "authentic" original form, fixed and reproduced in millions of identical copies on vinyl and CD and subject to copyright.[7] Of course, it is never performed live in the same manner either, just as no two performances of a Chopin sonata by the same pianist, or two oral history narratives by the same narrator are ever exactly identical. The difference, of course, is that in folk song and in oral history text and performance are inseparable, whereas the performance of the popular singer or the classical pianist is a mise-en-scène of a text that exists before and apart from the performance itself. As Cecil J. Sharp warned over a century ago, evolution and variation can also occur in "instrumentally composed" music; "nevertheless, these alterations can never . . . stray very far, for there is always a text to refer to and the critic to call attention to it and restrain the performer."[8] Most of those who hear Bob Dylan sing "Hard Rain" live have heard the record and recognize and appreciate (or deplore) the changes and inventions he introduces each time. When the song is performed by other artists—Pete Seeger, Joan Baez, the Staple Singers, Jimmy Cliff, Patti Smith in Stockholm or Lou Majaw in Shillong—their versions are perceived as "covers" that are inevitably measured against the standard of the original.[9] The impact of the Staple Singers' "wandering" or Jimmy Cliff's "brown-eyed" son derives exactly from their departure from the original "blue-eyed." Other than that, no one changes a word in the text—unless they get confused, like Patti Smith in Stockholm. It's a long song, and not easy to memorize.

Bob Dylan performed "Hard Rain" in concert 457 times between September 20, 1962, and July 17, 2017.[10] No wonder he gets bored if he has to do it the same way every time. For Dylan, never performing the same song in the same way twice is a way of resisting the idea that a concert is a ceremony of recognition; to him, instead, it is rather an occasion to explore (and to hear) something challenging and new ("Who comes to Bob Dylan music for pretty sounding music?"). On the other hand, he can afford to do this precisely because he knows that most people in the audience do not need to understand the words or follow the tune *in that moment* because *they already know them.* Like all denials, it evokes the denied object: another "it ain't me babe" thrown at the crowd and not always understood—no matter how hard he tries, for some fans "Dylan will always be Dylan."[11]

Like many American artists, from William Faulkner to Mark Twain, Bob Dylan resists the thought that a text, once written or recorded, is frozen forever in deadly motionlessness.[12] Once his songs are recorded in the studio, he says, "I don't want to hear them anymore. I know the songs. I'll play them, but I don't want to hear them on a record."[13] Yet, the shadow of the recorded original looms even in the act of performance, both because part of his audience would want to hear it that way and resents the changes and the alterations (while others celebrate them), and because Dylan himself is aware that the "text" exists behind his performance and is struggling against it.[14]

Part of what makes Bob Dylan different, then, is how he strives to be permanent as "text" and ephemeral as performance, thus placing himself where only an artist of the voice can stand, at the crossroads of the written or recorded artifact (the permanent past) and the oral performance (the evolving present and future). The live concert history of "Hard Rain," however, is unlike that of other Dylan classics. Songs like "High Water" or "Tangled Up in Blue" have a performance life of their own, distinct from the first recorded version; the search for meaning begins with the record but does not end there. The published version of "High Water" is more a starting point than a fixed reference.[15] "Tangled Up in Blue" tells two different stories, in the first person in the studio version on *Blood on the Tracks* (1975), in the third person in the Rome 1984 concert and the live album from that tour, *Real Live* (1985).[16] On the other hand, the live performances of "Hard Rain" add very little to the song, possibly because there is hardly anything to add. Dylan can change the sound, the phrasing, the tune, as in the acid-country rock version on *The Rolling Thunder Revue* (1975), or in the magnificent 2003 performance in New Orleans; but he never changes a word. In 2013, in St. Paul, not far from his native Hibbing, he mumbled the words until the song became almost unrecognizable (the applause does not start until the middle of the first verse; the audience recognized what he was singing only when they managed to make out the words) but he never changed a word.[17] He is not looking for new meanings but rather subtracting, denying the original "text" to avoid repeating it, nearly killing it to keep it alive.

Now, as Dylan's play of text and performance shows, the dynamics of both orality and writing hinge upon a contradiction between ideology and technology; as in a variant of the classical economics model, both value what they lack and prize the opposite of what they actually do. Oral cultures have an ideology of preservation precisely because they can preserve nothing outside the intangible and precarious space of memory. Singers and storytellers claim that they always sing and tell their stories and songs exactly as their ancestors did, but actually cannot help reshaping them every time; they claim tradition as permanence and practice it as evolution.

On the other hand, the cultures of writing, print, and mechanical reproduction of works of art are based on a practice of infinite repetition and proclaim an ideology of change; they produce and preserve millions of identical copies of books, records, and film, and seek the "new," the uniqueness and innovation of artistic vanguards, modernism, and postmodernism. Even the initial irreproducibility of performance is reversed, as performances are etched unchangeably on YouTube or live concert bootlegs. Thus, while the changes in oral tradition are largely involuntary and inevitable, those of the artistic vanguards are the result of deliberate choices. Dylan reshapes his songs each time precisely because he knows that they exist somewhere in the pristine immutable form of a text that no one will ever learn through "uncontaminated" oral transmission.

Both orality and writing strive against time. Ephemeral orality seeks to stop time; permanent writing seeks to set it in motion. Thus, both entertain a double reciprocal relationship with life and death. Orality affirms life with its motion and its relationship with the body and evokes death by its vanishing and disappearance. Writing, in turn, evokes death by its fixity, but denies it by its permanence and survival. Thus, like everything that lives, the ballad stays alive as long as it keeps changing, but is always one generation from extinction. When I met Carmela Luci in 1973, she was in her forties; Teresa Tacchini was born in 1914, Giovanna Nobili in 1920; Ada Barbonari, Vienna Di Lorenzo, Rosa Scorsolini, Argia Pitari, who all sang "Il testamento dell'avvelenato" for Valentino Paparelli's tape recorder in Umbria between 1974 and 1978, were 43, 50, 73, and 86 years old.[18] Maybe they are gone, maybe they forgot; maybe they passed it on to someone younger, maybe somewhere in the Apennines, in the Highlands, in the Appalachians, some adolescent is learning it right now. We don't know. Folk song has always been perceived as a "reliquy"[19] on the edge of extinction, but so far extinction has always been deferred.

Thanks to the mechanical reproducibility of music, there is no danger of this fate befalling "Hard Rain." Mark Edwards, an environmentalist photographer, tells an amazing story about it. In 1969, he was lost in the Sahara and rescued by a Tuareg nomad who took him to his camp, lit a fire by rubbing two sticks together, gave him a cup of tea, then turned on an old cassette player from which rose the voice of Bob Dylan singing "Hard Rain"[20]—not his latest live performance, but the version etched forever on record in New York in 1963. Should the song remain forgotten and unsung for centuries, there is always a chance that it may be retrieved and find a new life, like the rediscovered pages of a forgotten poet, on vinyl and CDs, in someone's attic, in archives and museums, or in the original matrix in the Columbia archives. What makes it different from the traditional ballad, of course, is that thanks to the time-stopping power of the technologies of the word,[21] we would have access to an "authentic" "original"—and only to that.

Yet, there is another turn of the screw. The technology of the voice that establishes once and forever the standard of "Hard Rain" is what enabled me, who has never heard them live, to listen to "Lord Randal" from the voice of Jeannie Robertson or Elizabeth Cronin. Of course, the performances etched in my precious vinyls are only the document of one of the countless times they sang it in their lives—like a still photograph of a moving object. Yet, it is far better than nothing, and it stays with me as a point of reference. Had I not had a tape recorder with me that day at Casalotti, we would not be talking about Carmela Luci. If we did not have "Lord Randal," "Il testamento dell'avvelenato," and "A Hard Rain's A-Gonna Fall" on tapes, audio files, records, and archives, we could not study and understand them as the lasting works of art they are.[22]

SPACE: THE HOME AND THE STAGE

I did not plan it that way, but I realize now that most of the names in this story are the names of women: the young women from Loveno, Teresa Tacchini, Jeannie Robertson, Elisabeth Cronin, Carmela Luci, Jean Ritchie, Sandra Mantovani, Betsy Miller, Giovanna Risolo, Giovanna Nobili, Ada Barbonari, Vienna Di Lorenzo, Rosa Scorsolini, Argia Pitari . . . The only males in this story are the "blue-eyed," "flowery," and "gentle" son—and Bob Dylan. Here, too, the dialectics of the home and the wilderness, the inside and the outside, help us understand the meaning of this gender imbalance. Historically, in fact, it was mainly males who claimed the privilege and risk of wandering into dark woods and highways of diamonds; errant knights are young men, princesses are locked in towers, women stay at home (as Bob Dylan reminds us ironically in "Sweetheart Like You").[23] Yet, ultimately the conflict in "Lord Randal" is represented by the contrast between two female roles, the mother and the lover, which makes the song especially significant for women bearers of the tradition—especially, as is often the case in recent times, elderly ones.

"A Hard Rain's A-Gonna Fall" and "Lord Randal" belong to cultural forms that entertain very different relationships with the private and the public space. Only a few months after writing it, Dylan presented "A Hard Rain's A-Gonna Fall" in public at Carnegie Hall; shortly afterward, he made it available to the whole world by means of a record that could be played on the radio and bought in stores—which is why I, too, had the privilege of hearing and playing it.

Folk songs, of course, are not sung only in private and not only by women. There are many public, near-professional forms—street singers, wedding musicians, improvisers—that are primarily male; and we have fine male versions of "Lord Randal," from Frank Proffit, the North Carolina tobacco farmer from whom Frank Warner recorded "Tom Dooley" in 1938, to Colum McDonagh of Galway, Ireland, who sang it in Gaelic for Alan Lomax, to the great Ewan MacColl—who learned it from his mother at home anyway.[24] Folk singing, however, is only occasionally a public performance, a show. It is done at home, at work, in company; the narrative ballad especially is transmitted mainly in the home and in women's spaces. Teresa Viarengo, the seamstress from Asti (Piedmont) who was a great Italian traditional ballad singer, never sang her incredible repertoire in public until she was "discovered" by Franco Coggiola, Gianni Bosio, and Roberto Leydi, and was always ill at ease when invited to perform on a folk festival stage.[25]

I recorded Carmela Luci at home. She sang "Il Testamento" with her mother (who was painfully out of key); fortunately, a few months later, Marco Müller, a youthful Circolo Gianni Bosio activist who would later become the director of the Venice Film Festival, went back and made a better recording. Carmela Luci had a wonderful voice, and we invited her to join folk singer Giovanna Marini in concert. She agreed, but the night she was supposed to appear she did not show up. She explained later that she would have loved to do it, but her husband would not allow her to perform in public.

I had a similar experience with the most beautiful female folk voice I have ever heard, Giuseppina Romano, a housewife from Isola Liri, Lazio. Once again, I recorded her at home, in the most intimate space—the bedroom where her mother (also a very good singer, this time) was lying ill. She had an unforgettable voice and a very interesting repertoire including a number of traditional ballads, so I went back a year later to invite her to sing in Rome at the Circolo Gianni Bosio folk club. To my surprise and chagrin, she seemed to have forgotten what she had sung for me just a year before, and even her voice was less free and more subdued. We could not figure out why; the only difference was that she had moved to a different space (from her village home to a factory gatehouse) and was in different company; the first time, she was at her mother's bedside, the second time she was in the presence of her husband.

DIGRESSION: KOLKATA, INDIA

Red graffiti on a wall at Jadavpur University, Kolkata, November 2016: "To the parliamentry left: Your road is rapidly aegin',"[26] signed SIF, Student Federation of India. It was more than half a century since *The Times They Are A-Changin'*, and Bob Dylan is still with us, with the same words that marked me for life, like the writings of the prophets on tenement halls, like the conclusions drawn on the walls of dime stores and bus stations. Around the corner, along the stairs, another Dylan (mis)quote on the wall: "All along the watchtower the princess kept the view . . ." and the drawing of a princess in a tower gazing into the distance.[27]

On the front of the building, lines from the first verse of "Which Side Are You On," written by Florence Reece during the dramatic miners' strike of 1932 in Harlan County, Kentucky (on the other side of the mountain where Jean Ritchie learned "Lord Randal" from her family). "They say in Harlan County / There are no neutrals there / You'll either be a union man / Or a thug for J. H. Blair." It is *the* song of the American labor movement, popularized by Pete Seeger, recorded and changed, as befits a folk song, by Ani DiFranco, Billy Bragg, and many others. That very day, I was on my way to teach a class on the oral history and memory of the Harlan County strike and its songs.[28]

Later, after my last class, Mrittiha Kalabar, a student who is also a folk singer, thanked me by singing a traditional Bengali folk song. Then another student, Sourav Saha, picked up his guitar and sang two songs he had written on the Indian student movement. The first song's title is "Hob Kolorob"; as Sourav Saha explained, "it literally means let there be polyphony, a sort of polyphony which is created from multiple voices of people singing together. This title has been derived from a popular Bengali song titled "Hok Kolorob" by a Bangla-deshi artist named Arnob.[29] The movement that took place in Jadavpur in 2014 has been named as the Hok Kolorob move-ment. I named my song after the movement since it was born out of the movement itself." This is the English translation he gave me, with clear echoes of Dylan's "Masters of War":

Oh friends, if you're listening to this song
Let me tell you a story, an epic in its own way
It was midnight and they were beaten up by mamata's
    [the state] army
An absolute autocracy of the uniform
And the war was about to begin (3 vv.)
A history in its making.

The other song he gave me is even more Dylanesque. It is the story of Rohit Vermula, a student who killed himself after the university canceled his scholarship to punish him for his polit-ical activism. Like many ballads and songs in Dylan's canon, this is another story of the young betrayed by the old, of teach-ers who "don't see the students" and don't realize that "they are invisibly bleeding." In another song, Sourav Saha recognized in his contemporary Rohit Vermula an avatar of Nishad Ekalavya, a character in Mahābhārata who was cheated and humiliated by his guru.[30]

Professor Indira Chowdhury, founder of the Oral History Association of India, explained later that in the mid-sixties they all knew these American protest songs. After all, I have heard the civil rights anthem "We Shall Overcome" sung in Hindi on a bus on the road to Bangalore, and in Bangla by a choir of children from Bangladesh in the popular neighborhood of Torpignattara in Rome.[31] It was in Kolkata in 1964 that Lou Majaw discovered "Blowin' in the Wind"; Sourav Saha had not been born yet, but he, too, belongs in this musical and poetic tradition:

> I think ["Hard Rain"] is one of the most imaginatively powerful songs that he has written. The word "blue-eyed son" is the most magical word that I find in the entire song. The first time I head Bob Dylan I was 15. My father used to bring home the cassettes of his concerts, and it felt good to see how he does subtle musical changes to manipulate emotions from the stage. During my school days we used to have a band of our own where we covered songs like "All Along the Watchtower," "Blowin' in the Wind," "Tambourine Man" and many others. I had written a couple of Bengali songs which were very much inspired by the kind of performative style that he devised for himself. It is a trilingual song. Hindi, Bengali and English. I used these three languages in orchestrating three different sections of the song. I was 18 then. I had visited a puja pandal in the month of September when durgapuja is held. We were amused to discover that the locality played Bob Dylan songs during the puja which was completely shocking for us.[32]

SPACE: CONTINENTS

How did Bob Dylan, who has never set foot in India, become a model and a source of inspiration for a young man from Bengal?

How did his voice travel from Greenwich Village to Jadavpur, to that coffee house in Shillong, Meghalaya, to that campfire in the middle of the Sahara? We know. It is the fortunate encounter between the worldwide circulation of the products of the culture industry and the shared passions of millions of young people all over the world. It is the internationalism of a globalization before the name, which enabled young rebels in India and in the United States (and me) to share the same words and the same music, without necessarily forgetting their own— indeed, as it was for Sourav Saha and for me, being driven to rediscover them.

On the other hand, in order to understand how it was possible for "Il testamento dell'avvelenato" to travel between Verona, Aberdeen, Cork County, and Viper, Kentucky, we need to use our imagination and envision on older, slower, but no less intense form of globalization. We must imagine a Europe at the dawn of modernity in which stories and songs traveled for centuries across the continent, carried, preserved, and changed osmotically by pilgrims, merchants, seasonal workers, travelers, beggars, soldiers, street singers, wandering clerics, hardly visible to the learned and the historians but always part of history and culture; we must imagine an Atlantic Ocean crossed both ways by migrants, deportees, mariners, renegades, and castaways, and an America that carried songs and stories westward as it expanded toward the Appalachians and beyond.

Here, again, Dylan stands at a crossroads: the one between *folk* and *popular*. Of course, this is only an abstract distinction; in reality, words and music travel back and forth all the time across this boundary, which is why the folk and the popular can meet and overlap in Bob Dylan and in "Hard Rain," as if it were the terminal leg of one journey and the beginning of another. Yet, the distinction has its methodological, logical uses. When we speak of "folk," we refer less to the origins of cultural texts than to the prevalent means and environment of their transmission and transformation—primarily the social world, the memory and the orality of the non-hegemonic classes, through the interactive contribution of myriads of subjects across time and space. When we speak of the "popular," we refer to texts that originate in the centers of the culture industry and achieve a quick and pervasive (if often epheremeal) circulation; the members of the audience interact by buying the products and interpreting their meaning, but without changing the letter. Thus, "Lord Randal" is the same on two continents, but it is different in each village; "A Hard Rain's A-Gonna Fall" can mean different things to each listener, precisely thanks to the fact that, all over the world, the words and the notes remain the same. And both processes are necessary and beautiful.

TESTAMENTS

At the end of "Hard Rain," the mother of Dylan's blue-eyed son asks him what he plans to do now, and, in his way, he also makes his will: "I'll know my song well before I start singin'." His will is the testament and testimony of an artist or a prophet, which is why it cannot be improvised but must be learned and memorized, because it is a universal message that all humankind must share.

Lord Randal's will, instead, keeps changing in history and in space, from time to time, from village to village. Take the version of "Il Testamento dell'avvelenato" collected by Giovanni Bolza in Northern Italy around 1860, and recorded by Sandra Mantovani in 1963:

> Cosa lassé alla vostra mama, figliol mio caro fiorito e
>   gentil?
> Cosa lassé alla vostra mama?
> Ghe lasso il mio palasso, signora mama, mio core sta mal,
> ghe lasso il mio palasso, ohimè ch'io moro, ohimè.
> (What will you leave to your mother, my dear, flowery
>   and gentle son?
> I leave her my palace, alas, my heart is in pain,
> I leave her my palace, alas, I am dying.)

Compare with the version from Calabria, Southern Italy, as sung in 1973 by Carmela Luci in Rome:

> 'T a mamma chi'nci 'assate, figlio caro mio gentil
> 'T a mamma chi'nci 'assate, gentile mio cavalier?
> Lascio l'occhi per chiangiri, mamma lo core mi sento ca mor
> Lascio l'occhi per chiangiri, ahimé ch'io morerò.
> (What will you leave your mother, my dear gentle son?
> I leave her eyes to cry with, I feel that my heart is dying
> I leave her eyes to cry with, alas, I am going to die.)

A palace in nineteenth-century Northern Italy, life-long mourning and tears in the twentieth-century South. In different historical and social contexts, each legate defines in symbolic terms the social role of the heirs; thus, if we follow the changes of the song across time and space, we find the traces of a social history of the family in the Western world. In the Northern version, possibly closer to the one heard in seventeenth century Verona, the legates are palaces, coaches, horses, as befits an aristocratic family in the Renaissance city of *Romeo and Juliet* and *The Two Gentlemen of Verona* reinvented by William Shakespeare through Giraldi Cintio—either because the song may have been sung also in courtly ambients, or because that is where the folk imagination locates it. As the song travels through time and social space, it becomes the near-exclusive property of poorer and more rural folks. Thus, the more recent Southern version sets the story in an environment of rural poverty where there is hardly anything to make a will about—the brother inherits a rifle to hunt for his food, the mother the tears that stand for those eternally black-clad traditional Southern widowhoods. In the nineteenth-century North, the hero is poisoned by his "lady"; in twentieth-century South, by his "zita" (a dialect word for "fiancée"); the Northern household includes "the help," the Southern only one "servant." In 1974, near Como, the first part of Teresa Tacchini's version was almost identical to the version collected in the same area a century before by Giovanni Bolza, but the testament was different: the mother no longer inherits the coach and horses, but the roads of the world, like the poor widows of the South. In time, then, the song has been brought closer to home; rather than an imagined courtly environment, it reflects the experience of its singers, rural mountaineers and landless peasants in lands of emigration who have hardly ever seen, let alone owned, a coach and horses anyway. Indeed, the only things that don't change concern the weakest members of the household: daughters always inherit some form of dowry to get married on; servants inherit "the broom to sweep with" in Calabria or "the way to the church" in Lombardy. In many British versions, both the servants and the younger brothers inherit "the roads of the world," an echo of the feudal laws that, to keep the property intact, turn younger siblings into errant knights.

On the basis of about two hundred Italian and Anglophone versions I have indexed, I would suggest that by and large, and making allowances for the vagaries of memory and the difficulty of forcing oral tradition into schemes and formulas, the structure is this: the surviving authority figure (most often a brother, sometimes the mother, seldom the father) inherits some kind of property that changes according to local conditions (a palace in Como, a plantation in North Carolina); the mother inherits symbols of status; younger brothers inherit means of support (money, hunting guns and dogs, ships a-sea, working tools); the sisters inherit some form of dowry; the lower members of the household (servants, cadet siblings in Britain, widows in the rural Italian South) inherit poverty, the life on the road, and the solace of religion.

We recognize then the confluence and interaction of a principle of order and stability (the continuity of social memory) and a principle of variation and change (different roles, different symbols, in different contexts). There is, however, another subject whose inheritance remains the same. This is the final verse as sung by Ada Barbonari and Rosa Scorsolini in Umbria in the 1970s:

Che gli lasci alla tua dama, figliol mio caro servito e gentil
Che gli lasci alla tua dama?
Il fuoco pe' brucialla, la forca pe'impiccalla, la corda pe'
strozzalla.
(What will you leave your lady, my dear gentle and
respected son?
Fire to burn her, the gallows to hang her, the rope to
strangle her.)

And Ewan MacColl, straddling the English-Scottish border:

What will you leave your sweetheart, my son?
What will you leave your sweetheart, my bonnie young
man?
The tow and the halter that hangs on yon tree
And there let her hang for the poisoning of me.[33]

POETICS: CONDENSATION

The ballad, then, is a folk song that tells a story. Yet not all
narrative songs are ballads; a ballad is a song that tells a story
in a certain way. In musical terms, a ballad, like most folk
song genres, "is always sung to a rounded melody"[34] and usually sung unaccompanied. It is always in strophic form; in the
Anglo-Saxon world, usually four-line verses rhyming the even
lines, often with a refrain between verses or a "burden" between
lines (in "Lord Randal," the two burdens—"my darling young
son" and "mother make my bed soon"—are repeated after each

line). Usually, each metric and musical unit, each line and each verse, is also a self-contained semantic unit; there is no enjambement.

What makes the ballad different, however, is the way it tells the story. Oral cultures are confronted with two distinct aspects of time: the diachrony of memory and the sinchrony of performance. Thus, orality functions somehow like the heart, by systole and diastole, contraction and expansion. On the one hand, it selects and hones its "texts" so they can be enclosed and concentrated within the limits of social memory; on the other hand, it expands them in digressions, repetitions, chorus, burden, and anaphora, allowing them to "breathe" in the more leisurely time of performance in order to extend the pleasure of talking, singing, and listening, and to test the audience's reception and facilitate memorization. All oral historians have experienced the way narrators will handle narrative time by skipping or skimming over long stretches of time and in turn dwelling over and over on apparently secondary details or specific episodes.[35]

The ballad's narrative style is a result of this process. The story is honed down to the essential minimum, stressing dramatic situation over narrative continuity or character definition; the action is focused on a single critical or final scene, omitting the events leading up to it, minimizing comments or descriptions, and leaving performers and listeners to interpret the meaning of the story for themselves.[36] There are no moral commentaries, judgments, or explanations; the story is told objectively, in the third person or in dialogue, minimizing the narrative voice or eliminating it altogether (as in both "Lord Randal" and "Hard Rain"). We are never told why the "lady" poisons the hero, but it does not matter. As it goes through the countless transitions of the oral tradition, the song sheds all superfluous detail and turns "characters" into archetypes, symbols, and abstract functions. The ballad is not about a specific naive young man who goes out to hunt into the wildwood (or up to protest in Genoa), but *all* of them. We don't know why Lord Randal or the blue-eyed son leave home, we do no not stay with them until the end. Both the ballad and Dylan's song only tell the story through the dramatic scene of the mother-son dialogue, and leave us to imagine the rest (indeed, "Hard Rain" does not describe the hero's visions and encounters, but his *memory* of them).

Folk music and poetry inhabit social environments in which people must do the best they can with limited means, both materially and culturally. The fewer the words, the deeper and more powerful the resonance around them: the "wildwood" in "Lord Randal" evokes and suggests all the many horrors and mysteries that the blue-eyed son encounters in his journey and all the dangers that we are able to imagine. Let us take another example. In September 1961, at the Gaslight Café in Greenwich Village, Bob Dylan sang one of the most beloved murder ballads in the American canon, "Pretty Polly." The makeshift recording included in the *Live at the Gaslight* album and available on YouTube[37] seems to begin halfway through the performance; it misses the first few verses, in which Sweet William asks Pretty Polly to go with him to see something before they get married. They walk into a lonesome nocturnal landscape, until Pretty Polly begins to worry. Here is where the recording begins:

> Oh Willie, oh Willie, I'm scared of your ways
> Oh Willie, oh Willie, I'm scared of your ways
> I'm scared you will lead my poor body astray
>
> Pretty Polly, Pretty Polly, you guessed just about right
> Well, Polly, Pretty Polly, you guessed just about right
> For I dug on your grave the best part of last night

The ballad has a long history, but, unlike "Lord Randal," we can identify occasion, origin, and an original text: a mid-1700s broadside ballad entitled "The Gosport Tragedy," a copy of which is still preserved in the British Library's Roxburghe Collection. In thirty-nine four-line verses, the song tells the story of a sailor who murdered his pregnant lover in such accurate detail that folklorist David Fowler was able to reconstruct the identity of the characters, the date of the event, and the name of the ship.[38] As it was popularized in England and Scotland on printed broadsides and in music halls, the song was also honed down by oral tradition; as Ewan McColl and Peggy Seeger wrote, "generations of singers used their creative power to turn its four-line stanzas of doggerel into dramatic three-line verses."[39] As always, the process consisted of condensation/sistole on one side (from the 156 lines in the British broadside to less than 20 in most American versions) and expansion/diastole on the other (repetitions, instrumental breaks that prolong the performance). Topical details are abolished, dialogue prevails over narrative voice, there is no trace of motivations, place, or context. In "The Gosport Tragedy," the sailor kills the pregnant girl to keep from having to marry her; in "Pretty Polly" as Bob Dylan knew it, she asks him why he is killing her and he says there is no time to talk about it. Simply, just as the "true love" kills Lord Randal *because* she is his fiancée, so does Sweet William kill Pretty Polly *because* men kill women, period. A sordid news story has been turned into the archetype of an ancient and persisting violence.

If we compare Lord Randal's "wildwood" with Bob Dylan's "sad forests," however, we realize that there is also another kind of poetics at work. The wood in the folk song is "wild" by default, its symbolic connotations are included in its objective denotation. But how can a forest be "sad"? Here, Dylan is using a device that belongs less to ballad poetics than to the Romantic tradition: the so-called pathetic fallacy, in which natural objects share and reflect the feelings and emotions of the human observer and participant.

Ballad poetics make very little use of adjectives because they have no room and no need for the description of emotions. There are only two adjectives in "Lord Randal": "true" and "wild." "Wild" is both symbolic and functional; since Homeric times, the dialectics of memory and performance are facilitated by the use of fixed formulaic pairs in which adjectives are only a fixed appendix of nouns, so that the sea is always wine-dark, the dawn is always rosy-fingered, woods are always wild, lovers are always "true" (even when they end up poisoning you), children are darling, and innocent wanderers are blue-eyed.[40]

In "Hard Rain," descriptive adjectives abound in the first verse (misty, crooked, sad, dead), but fade away in the rest of the song. The narrator lists what he has seen and heard with the seemingly neutral, detached tones of the ballad, which does not describe or prescribe emotions but includes them in the mere naming of the objects. In the second verse, aside from the denotative "white" and "black," we find only two adjectives that are so formulaic as to be practically pleonastic: all "wolves" are by definition "wild" and all "children" are "young." There are no more adjectives until the "deepest dark forests" and the "damp dirty prison," in which they function, once again, as alliterative formulaic appendixes to the nouns.

"Hard Rain," however, breaks from the ballad style by expanding the traditional four-line form into verses of variable length (8, 10, 10, 9, 15). Yet precisely because the verses are not all of the same length, the principle of the rounded melody is transferred from verse to line: "What makes it so infernally powerful and demanding is the fact that V—I (the last two chords in the repeated sequence in the middle of each verse) is a standard resolution of a song. It signifies an ending, not a mid-point." This is probably part of what Bob Dylan meant when he said that each verse might be a separate song: poetically, as the matrix of another text; musically, as self-sufficient units of sound.[41]

In this way, then, Dylan retains—as he does in most of his work—the folk coincidence of metric, musical, semantic units.[42] In the shadow of impending nuclear doom, he says, he did not know how much time he had for writing songs, so he concentrated everything he knew in this one. The song seems to end at each line, and then it begins again, so that we do not know when it will really end, and the lines and visions keep coming, the verse dilates, and the rain is always about to fall and never does—perhaps because it has fallen already, and we have neither eyes to see it nor ears to hear it.

POETICS—EXPANSION

Memory concentrates inward, performance expands outward. Alessandro Carrera writes, "What makes folk music arcane and alchemic is the enchantment of repetition, in the chain of words that are turned into a single, long line by the repetition of the melody."[43] I might hesitate to call arcane and alchemic my contemporaries Carmela Luci, Giuseppina Romano, or Jean Ritchie, two homemakers and a miner's daughter that I had the pleasure of meeting. Yet, from the point of view of poetic and musical form, Carrera is absolutely right; on the one hand, repetition facilitates memorization and remembrance, and on the other, it expands the time and pleasure of performance and secures contact and reception. As is often the case, function generate aesthetics; while repetition is functionally necessary for contact and memory,[44] its hypnotic returns also generates an enchanted time out of time sustained by a poetics of recurring sounds—alliteration, consonance, rhyme, anaphora.

Both "Lord Randal" and "Hard Rain" make ample use of alliteration. "Il Testamento dell'avvelenato" has no rhyme or consonance, but is rife with alliteration, like the *s*, *m*, and *a* in

Bolza's version ("so sta' dalla mia dama, signora mama, mio core sta mal") or the *b*, *w*, and *m* in Ewan McColl's "Lord Randal" ("I've been to the wildwood, mother make my bed"). "Hard Rain," in turn, teems with alliteration, especially in the first and last verses, as if complementing the sound of the music with language as sound.[45]

The structural poetic device in "Hard Rain," however, is anaphora, the repetition of an element at the beginning of each line:

> I heard the sound of a thunder, it roared out a warnin'
> Heard the roar of a wave that could drown the whole
> world
> Heard one hundred drummers whose hands were
> a-blazin'
> Heard ten thousand whisperin' and nobody listenin'
> Heard one person starve, I heard many people laughin'
> Heard the song of a poet who died in the gutter
> Heard the sound of a clown who cried in the alley . . .

Both "Hard Rain" and the anglophone variants of "Lord Randal" open with an anaphora in *wh* (where, what, who). In the ballad, the anaphora returns in the second part, when the hero makes his will:

> Cosa le lasci alle tue sorelle . . . E le lassu la dota puntata
> Cosa le lasci a li toi cocchieri . . . E le lascio la carrozza
> Cosa le lasci al tuo padre . . . E le lascio di nuovo la
> corona alla testa.[46]

And:

> It's what will you will to your father . . .
> It's what will you will to your brother . . . [47]

In "Lord Randal," the making of the will is structured on one of the most popular forms of anaphora in the folk tradition, the so-called "climax of relatives," which expands the performance by adding family members and verses ad libitum.[48] A classic spiritual that Bob Dylan knows and quotes: "You've got to walk that lonesome valley," and then "father's got to walk . . . mother's got to walk . . . brother's got to walk . . ." as long as the singer's imagination and the listeners' patience last.[49] Or Bob Dylan's own "Maggie's Farm": "I ain't gonna work on Maggie's farm no more . . . I ain't gonna work for Maggie's brother no more . . . I ain't gonna work for Maggie's pa . . . I ain't gonna work for Maggie's ma . . ."[50]

The function of anaphora is both expansion and cohesion: each line is a self-contained musical and semantic unit, but the elements repeated from line to line connect each unit to the whole. This function is underlined by the symmetry of related formulas in the same metric and musical position: "black branch/ white ladder"; "white man/ black dog"; "The song of a poet/ The sound of a clown"; "Young woman / young girl"; "Wounded in love / wounded in hatred." In the absence of rhymes, cohesion is reinforced by the insisted use of the verbal *in'* form (four times in the third verse), which in turn becomes part of an extended play of lines ending with a consonance in *n*.[51]

Now, in oral tradition, all devices born of necessity are turned into aesthetic opportunities. Anaphora, for instance, can serve merely as connection and expansion; but it can also generate a mounting tension that culminates in a dramatic climax. Thus, the formulaic sequence of verbs in the first verse—"stumbled, walked, stepped, been"—suggests the progression from a hesitant step to a firm stand. The anxious series of questions—where have you been, what did you eat—in "Lord Randal" culminates in the revelation of the murder, while the anaphoric and often alliterate series of legates prepares the final vengeance and curse: "The *h*ighest *h*ill to *h*ang her", "A rope from *h*ell to *h*ang her", "la *f*orca pe'mpiccarla, la *f*iamma pe' brucialla, la *f*une pe' strozzalla."[52] In "Hard Rain," the climax is the return at the end of each verse of the (expected) prophecy of doom—a crescendo ("It's a hard, it's a hard, it's a hard, it's a hard"), a long moment of suspension (" it's a hard raiiiiin"), and the end.

Ultimately, "Hard Rain's" dramatic impact depends on the relationship of voice and time. The climax returns at the end of each verse but, because verses have an unpredictable number of lines, we never really know when it will fall: the rain is both announced and unexpected. Those of us who have already heard the song, or read the title on the record's sleeve, know how it ends. But if we could for a moment place ourselves in the position of one who hears "Lord Randal" for the first time, does not know the story, and goes through the double shock of the discovery of the murder and the punishment of the murderer, then the announcement of the hard rain that is going to fall would hit us at the end of the first verse with the power of those final couplets that Italian folk poets aptly call "the hammer blow."

JOURNEYS

In the early sixties, Allen Ginsberg heard "A Hard Rain's A-Gonna Fall" for the first time. He said later that he had wept with joy at the realization that the baton—the vision, the language—was now being relayed to another generation.[53]

When he wrote "Hard Rain," Bob Dylan was also beginning to seek other roads and other tongues. He was growing out of the "stagey panhandle dialect"[54] that was part of the vagabond orphan mask he put on when he first came to New York. Certain vernacular quirks in *Freewheelin'*—the *if'n, knowed/road* in "Don't Think Twice It's All Right," *lookit here buddy* in "Bob Dylan's Blues," the deliberately clownish *thumpin'/sumpin'* in "Talkin' World War III Blues" (that he possibly lifted from Little Richard's "Baby Face"[55])—were being gradually winnowed out in politically engaged songs like "Blowin' in the Wind" or "Masters of War." In "Hard Rain," Dylan still uses certain colloquial forms—the emphatic *a-*, the dropped *g* (a-gonna, a-bleedin', a-blazin', a-fallin')—but is beginning to shed the vernacular mask, perhaps to exchange it for new ones, but with a different language.

In Greenwich Village, Dylan breathed other voices, befriended Allen Ginsberg, attended beat poetry readings and theater performances; on the other hand, since his time in Minneapolis, he had been aware of "poetry on the page. . . the French guys, Rimbaud and François Villon."[56] Villon's image of the poet as outcast and outlaw may have influenced Dylan's later persona, but the crucial influence is Rimbaud. He claimed at times that he had never read him,[57] but in a relatively short time Rimbaud was to replace or supplement Woody Guthrie as a source of inspiration. As Alessandro Carrera writes, "Beyond its Child-ballad motions, 'A Hard Rain's A-Gonna Fall' revealed Rimbaud's 'Le Bateau ivre' as its deep-lying subtext."[58]

The first connection Carrera notes is, in fact, the use of anaphora: "Je sais les cieux crevant en éclairs"; "J'ai vu le soleil bas, taché d'horreurs mystiques,"; "J'ai rêvé la nuit verte aux neiges éblouies. . . ."; "J'ai suivi . . . j'ai heurté . . . j'ai vu. . . ." Dylan's use of anaphora is not a functional necessity: he certainly does not need anaphora to expand a song—see "Desolation Row," "Sad Eyed Lady of the Lowlands," "Tempest," all the way to his recent "Murder Most Foul"; furthermore, recording technology permits us to extend and repeat the pleasure of listening indefinitely anyway. Rather than a compositional support as in the oral tradition, then, anaphora in "Hard Rain" is, like in Rimbaud's "Le Bateau ivre," an aesthetic choice.

Dylan might have encountered anaphora as poetic device before Rimbaud, in the American tradition of Walt Whitman lists and catalogs, in the Chicago of another poet and folk singer, Carl Sandburg,[59] and, of course, in the work of Allen Ginsberg, another poet who constantly explored the role of the voice and would eventually record with Bob Dylan himself.[60] Nor should we forget the influence of Woody Guthrie's own poetic experiments and the cumulative stream of consciousness passages in his novel *Bound for Glory* (1943). But it was with his discovery of Rimbaud that Dylan became fully aware of the visionary possibilities in this figure of speech that is to language what riffs are to music, an obsessively hammered interrogation and a resolution that opens and closes in one motion.

The consonances and dissonances between Dylan and Rimbaud, however, go further than that. The first thing one notices on reading "Le Bateau ivre" with Dylan in mind is the echo between the "Fleuves impassibles" in the first line of Rimbaud's poem, and the "sad forests" in the first verse of "Hard Rain." Both assign a kind of subjectivity to the natural world; in Dylan, however, the forests refect the narrator's state of mind, while in Rimbaud the impassive river suggests nature's indifference to human destinies. The two narrators, in fact, journey into very different landscapes. Dylan's blue-eyed son encounters sights and beings that we do not encounter in our everyday experience— or, perhaps, we do meet but don't recognize until we journey with Dylan and Rimbaud into a surreal territory where ordinary experience is reshaped in a vision of "mystic horrors." Yet, while "Le Bateau ivre" teems with adjectives and revels in myriad colors, the only colors in "Hard Rain" are black and white, and adjectives are few and formulaic. Dylan has not yet begun to explore the sensory estrangement of symbolist poetry: time is still linear (as opposed to what he will do later with "Tangled Up in Blue"), there is no synesthesia (as opposed to the "Rimbaud's "green night"), the hero sees visible objects, hears audible sounds, meets physical persons.

Actually, the narrative voice in "Hard Rain" is halfway between "Le Bateau ivre" and "Lord Randal." On the one hand, while Rimbaud's poem is a monologue in one voice, "Hard Rain" and "Lord Randal" are dialogues. On the other hand, however, while in "Lord Randal" the two voices share the song's space equally, in "Hard Rain" the mother's is there only to ask the questions that prompt the telling of the story. In this sense, then, Dylan's blue-eyed son, "an heir of Romanticism" ("Blake's and Keats's, for a start")[61], is closer to Rimbaud's lyric self: another Romantic artist whose lonely heroic demise stands in opposition and denunciation of the world.

Listen to some of "Hard Rain's" more conventional lines—the dying poet, the weeping clown,[62] and then the thousand whispering with nobody listening, the talkers whose tongues are all broken: much of "Hard Rain" is about silence. The mission of the artist, alone and unheard, is to take a stand against silence, with his imagination and voice: his testament and testimony from the mountaintop is a legacy of thought, vision, voice, and music. He will know his song well and, singing, sink down to his fate.[63]

Chapter Three

TALKING ATOMIC BLUES

WHAT HAVE THEY DONE TO THE RAIN?

It's not about atomic rain, Bob Dylan says: "It's only a hard rain." And yet—how can rain be *hard*?[1] A hard rain, after all, is nothing but hail, tough but not the end of the world. Among many possible Italian equivalents, Alessandro Carrera chooses "ardua"—difficult, hard to explain, interpret, understand (and *ardua* does sound like *hard*). Perhaps, however, the point is less the intrinsic quality of this rain than the consequence of its impact. In the folk revival circles in which he was moving at the time, Dylan might have heard about *Hard-Hitting Songs for Hard-Hit People*, a book compiled and edited in the late thirties by Alan Lomax, Pete Seeger, and Woody Guthrie, which was being retrieved for publication by Irwin Silber, the editor of *Sing Out!*, which first published "Hard Rain."[2] A hard-hitting rain, a rain that kills and destroys? Or, perhaps, the "hard" rain is like the "sad" forest, endowed with a subjectivity of its own—after all, it is less a natural event than a product of human madness. Hard as pitiless, cruel, like the "hard-hearted" Barbara Allen of the ballad that Bob Dylan had sung at the Gaslight in 1962, performed dozens of times in concert, and used as his inspiration for "Scarlet Town"?[3]

Indeed, Bob Dylan's hard rain also sounds like an answer to, or a dialogue with "the gentle rain" in another song that he must have heard from Joan Baez in 1961–1962. It was written by Malvina Reynolds, the author of "Little Boxes," who had a special talent for saying very tough things in the softest of languages; no wonder Joan Baez dubbed "What Have They Done to the Rain" as "the gentlest protest song I know. It doesn't protest gently," she said, "but it sounds gentle."[4]

> Just a little rain falling all around
> The grass lifts its head to the heavenly sound
> Just a little rain, just a little rain
> What have they done to the rain?

No looming apocalypse, but a soft catastrophe in progress that has been killing us with kindness for a long time ("the gentle rain that falls for years"). Not the surreal terrors and dangers of an unknown hostile world, but the familiar images of a garden, a child, the grass. One does not need to travel on crooked highways and dead oceans to encounter the apocalypse: it's already here, at home with us. Malvina Reynolds's rain, too, is the result of human actions (what have *they* done to the rain?) and is therefore also endowed with a subjectivity of a kind; it is gentle because it kills us gently, with a whimper, not with a bang.

Malvina Reynolds's rain is our time; Bob Dylan's, as Alessandro Carrera explains, is the rain "at the end of time."[5] In 1962, however, the end of time was both a biblical prophecy and a present historical possibility. Bob Dylan was already exploring the eternal and the universal, but he never lost touch with the timely and the visible: "I didn't want to sing anything that was unspecific. Unspecific things have no sense of time."[6] The apocalypse of which he sings is both the end of time and the near future looming upon the present. When he insisted that "Hard Rain" is not about the nuclear nightmare, Dylan distanced himself from the image of the "topical" singer who sings the news; yet, in the same interview, he said that he wrote the song at the time of the Cuban missile crisis. The song is both timely and timeless. In fact, he insisted all the time that one does not need a single moment in time in order to be haunted by the fear of nuclear death. A key to the history and meaning of the sixties, "A Hard Rain's A-Gonna Fall" is not *only* about the bomb, but the bomb is the historical datum that sustains a broader vision of the future. We will discuss the vision later; meanwhile, let us talk about the bomb.

ATOM BOMB BABY

"In 1951," Bob Dylan recalls, "I was going to grade school. One of the things we were trained to do was to hide and take cover under our desks when the air-raid sirens blew because the

Russians could attack us with bombs . . . As if this could save us from the bombs dropping. The threat of annihilation was a scary thing."[7] I was taught to do the same as late as 1961, during my year as a foreign exchange student in a Los Angeles high school. Growing up in the fifties meant growing up with cold war in the air and the end of the world in our sights, without even knowing from where it would come:

> But now we got weapons
> Of the chemical dust
> If fire them we're forced to
> Then fire them we must
> One push of the button
> And a shot the world wide
> And you never ask questions
> When God's on your side[8]

If he says so, it must be true, no matter how unlikely, that Bob Dylan wasn't thinking of the bomb when he wrote "A Hard Rain's A-Gonna Fall." It is a fact, however, that he was thinking about it often, before and after. He had already composed and recorded "Hard Rain" when he joined Pete Seeger at the 1963 Newport Folk Festival to present another song he had written about it: "You fallout shelter sellers / Can't get in my door / Not now or no other time."[9]

Quiet as its kept, in that same 1961 in which I was taught to hide under my school desk to save me from the atom bomb, Bob Dylan was demonstrating against this nonsense in the streets of New York, along with fellow folksingers Gil Turner and Happy

Traum (the latter was arrested and spent three months in jail).[10] At the height of the Cold War, every American citizen was supposed to have quick access to a fallout shelter; the omni-present yellow and black signals that directed citizens to the nearest shelter are an icon for an era and a state of mind. Mark Spoelstra, a folksinger who often performed with Bob Dylan in those days, recognized them as "a hole for the souls of your friends and mine." "Of course a certain percentage has to go / But I won't be the one to die," he sang; and as long as we keep making missiles "daddy will have a job," at least until "we can all lie down and die / then daddy won't have to work anymore."[11]

"I was in Kansas, Phillipsbug or Maryville, I think," Bob Dylan recalls: "I was going through some town out there and they were making this bomb shelter right out of town, one of these sort of Coliseum-type things, and there were construction workers and everything. . . . As I watched them building, it struck me sort of funny when they would concentrate so much on digging a hole underground when there were so many other things they should do in life."[12]

> I will not go down under the ground
> 'Cause somebody tells me that death's comin' round
> An' I will not carry myself down to die
> When I go to my grave my head will be high
> Let me die in my footsteps
> Before I go down under the ground.[13]

There are better things to do than spend our lives digging our graves. Before I go down under the ground, Dylan proclaims,

I want to drink the waters from mountain streams, smell the wildflowers, see the craters, the canyons, the waterfalls where the land meets the sun. Bob Dylan's "Let Me Die in My Footsteps" is a proud call for dignity in the face of death, with echoes of Woody Guthrie's "This Land Is Your Land" or Cole Porter's "Don't Fence Me In"; before the end, hold your head high, fill your eyes with the beauty and openness of the American land.

Bob Dylan recorded "Let Me Die in My Footsteps" for *Freewheelin'*, but in the end it was dropped from the album. It could not coexist with "A Hard Rain's A-Gonna Fall," not only because there was no space for two epic songs on the same subject, but, most importantly, because their respective moods were incompatible; there was no room for flowers, waters, and skies in the looming apocalypse. The Bob Dylan who writes "Let Me Die in My Footsteps" is like the blue-eyed boy before he sets out on his journey, expecting the beauty of nature instead of tragedy and death. Perhaps the true "mouth of a graveyard" is the fallout shelter. Or is the call in "Let Me Die in My Footsteps" to seek beauty and poetry in nature before the apocalypse, the content of the song that the blue-eyed son sings before he starts sinking? Both, anyway, will die standing.

"There's better things to do / Than blow the world in two," sang Peggy Seeger and Ewan MacColl. Bob Dylan's anti-nuclear songs are a part of an oral and musical history of the Cold War years that spans the whole gamut from anti-nuclear protest songs to anthems in praise of the bomb. In the same year Dylan composed "Hard Rain," Pete Seeger put Nazim Hikmet's poem on a child killed at Hiroshima to the music of the Scottish ballad "The Great Seal of Shule Skerry."

I come and stand at every door
But no one hears my silent tread
I knock and yet remain unseen
For I am dead, for I am dead.

I'm only seven although I died
In Hiroshima long ago
I'm seven now as I was then
When children die, they do not grow.[14]

Always an internationalist, Pete Seeger translated a song from the Japanese anti-nuclear movement, "We shall never allow another atom bomb to fall." "In the garden where we buried the ashes of our loved ones," the song says, "flowers now grow."[15] Seeger also imported to the United States the songs of the British CND (Campaign for Nuclear Disarmament), like Alex Comfort's "One Man's Hands." "One man's hands can't tear a prison down, two men's hands can't tear a prison down," one man's hands can't ban the bomb, can't roll the union on, "but if two and two and fifty make a million / we'll see that day come round."[16]

The message is always the same: never more, it's up to us, and we can do it. The power and the weakness of these songs reside in their hopefulness. On the one hand, the idea that human beings united can be stronger than the atom is an invitation to solidarity, to join forces and act; on the other, the implicit optimism seems to dilute the magnitude of the danger and the radicalism of the protest itself. The message of Dylan's "A Hard Rain's A-Gonna Fall" and "Let Me Die in My Footsteps" was both more fatalistic and more radical: you can't hide from the bomb, not even under the ground.[17]

Bob Dylan said once that the atom bomb, the possible extinction the human race, underlies the music of his generation. Artists like Carl Perkins, Elvis Presley, Chuck Berry, Jerry Lee Lewis, were all "fast and furious," always pushing against the limit, because they were "atom-bomb-fueled."[18] Those were the years in which the bomb was a metaphor for all sorts of power, an "explosive" two-piece bathing suit could be named after a nuclear-test site, Bikini, while rockabilly and country singers exorcized the fear of doom by singing the praises of a "Radioactive Mama" and an "Atom Bomb Baby," who was "a million times hotter than TNT."[19] Bob Dylan was not the first to perceive the biblical connotations of the bomb; they recur obsessively in all musical genres of the time. In 1947, the Golden Gate Quartet revisited Genesis with a wordplay between Adam and Atom, Evil and Eve: "we're sitting on the edge of doom," they warned, and unless we "break up the romance" between Atom and Evil, we will soon "fall down and go boom boom boom."[20]

The Adam/Atom homophony is also the source of the black humor in Vern Partlow's classic "Talking Atomic Blues" (1946). First recorded by Pete Seeger in 1948, it was performed by Sam Hinton at the same 1963 Newport Folk Festival topical song concert in which Bob Dylan sang "Ye Playboys and Playgirls" and "With God on Our Side" with Pete Seeger and Joan Baez.[21] In this song, Adam\Atom is reawakened by another "Evil," science's irresponsible hubris:

I'm gonna preach you-all a sermon 'bout Old Man Atom
I don't mean the Adam in the Bible datum
I don't mean the Adam that Mother Eve mated
I mean that thing that science liberated
The thing that Einstein says he's scared of
And when Einstein's scared, brother, I'm scared.[22]

While scientists are "splitting atoms," Vern Partlow mused, politicians are "splitting hairs" in the attempt to "extinguish \ Every darn atom that doesn't speak English."

But the atom's international, in spite of hysteria
Flourishes in Utah, also Siberia
And whether you're white, black, red or brown
The question is this, when you boil it down
To be or not to be!
That is the question.

"Peace in the world or the world in pieces," the song concludes. The biblical metaphor, however, is not necessarily pacifist. Indeed, atomic power—especially when it was still only in U.S. hands—could be read as another form of God's own power incarnated in a country with "God on [its] side." Only a few months after Hiroshima, the country duo Buchanan Brothers proclaimed that America's atomic power derived straight from "the hand of mighty God," while another country duo, Karl Davis and Harty Taylor, sang the praises of the nuclear omnipotence of the American God:[23]

Smoke and fire it did flow through the land of Tokyo
There was brimstone and dust everywhere
When it all cleared away there the cruel Japs did lay
The answer to our fighting boys' prayers
Yes, Lord, the answer to our fighting boys' prayers.

Bob Dylan himself, steeped in biblical culture, agreed that "If the Bible is right the world will explode."[24] All that is left, then, is to try to imagine what kind of world—if any—will remain after the explosion. The postwar decades teem with visions and nightmares of a postapocalyptic world in which few survivors roam in a landscape of destruction, such as Nevil Shute's *On the Beach* (1957) and its film version (Stanley Kramer, 1959), Nicholas Meyer's TV movie *The Day After* (1983), or Cormac McCarthy's novel *The Road* (2006). In 1963, the same year Bob Dylan recorded "Hard Rain," Harry Belafonte recorded Fran Minkoff and Fred Hellerman's tender and painful "Come Away Melinda" (1963), a postapocalyptic dialogue between a mother and a daughter. The child is excited about an old picture book she has found, with images of a pre-apocalypse world she has never seen: "Mammy, mammy, come and see / Mammy, come and look / There's four or five Melinda girls / Inside my picture book." "Come away, Melinda," the mother answers, in stoic resignation, "Come in and close the door / There were lots of little girls like you / Before they had the war."[25]

"Last night I was dreamin'," sang rock and roll pioneer Bill Haley: "the bomb went off," and all that remained were "thirteen women and only one man in town"; a dystopia masked as an ambiguous male utopia, with the narrator as the satisfied ruler of a harem of docile female survivors.[26] Bob Dylan, too, had a post-nuclear dream, a sort of counter narrative to Bill Haley's:

> Well, I spied a girl and before she could leave
> "Let's go and play Adam and Eve"
> I took her by the hand and my heart was thumpin'
> When she said, "Hey man, you crazy or sumpin'
> You see what happened last time they started."[27]

Genesis and Revelations, creation and apocalypse, in one verse: the end in the beginning. Dylan's "Talkin' World War III Blues" shares in the black humor of Vern Partlow's "Talking Atomic Blues," but not its moralizing finale. The form and tone are different from "Hard Rain," but the vision is just as disconsolate. In the dream, the narrator roams the streets of a deserted and paranoid city where they call him a Communist only because he speaks to a stranger, and the only sounds are the mechanical voices of the telephone hour signal ("when you hear the beep it will be three o' clock"), or the mock plaintive voice of Rock-a-day Johnny, a stand-in for all the inane teen idols of the cold-war era, "Tell Your Ma, Tell Your Pa / Our Love's A-gonna Grow Ooh-wah, Oo-wah." But time has stopped, three o'clock never comes, nobody grows up in the eternal adolescence of late fifties pop-rock music. Dylan's nightmare is not of the future but of the present; the apocalypse is already here, human beings are already lost and paranoid, all adrift in the same solitary dream. The song ends with one of Bob Dylan's most painful lines: "I'll let you be in my dream if I can be in yours." The world has already ended; the bomb is not a-gonna fall, it *is* falling, and we are living in the fallout.

HIGH WATERS

"But the bombs," a character in Don DeLillo's *Underworld* reminds us, "were not released. . . The missiles remained in the underwing carriages, the men came back and the targets were not destroyed."[28] This is perhaps why at some point we stopped worrying about the Bomb and began to hear "A Hard Rain's A-Gonna Fall" as a de-historicized vision of generic apocalypses. While the nuclear nightmare seemed to recede into the background, however, other possible ends of the world were looming on the horizon, revealing other implications, other visions and meanings, that kept Bob Dylan's song relevant in another phase of history.

Environmental photographer Mark Edwards tells how, after he heard "Hard Rain" in the desert from a Tuareg's battered cassette player, he conceived the project of illustrating each line of the song with images from current environmental disasters. This was the origin of the Hard Rain Project: an open exhibition, a book, and a DVD in which Mark Edwards accompanies Dylan's voice with images, creating "a third form that combines the stillness of a picture with the urgency of a ballad."[29] Some of the images are relatively expected, though quite appropriate: a desert of cut-down timbers ("sad forests"), the famous controversial image of the cormorant soaked in oil ("dead oceans"), children picking plastic refuse on a beach ("pellets of poison"), a bear on a shard of melting polar ice ("I'll stand on the ocean until I start sinking"), images of hunger, injustice, indifference ("where the people are many and their hands are all empty," "I heard one person starve, I heard many people laughing," "where hunger is ugly, where souls are forgotten"). Some are literal, like the child surrounded by wolves or sitting by a "dead pony." Rain appears always as driving, violent water falling on the poor. The most striking image, however, is that of the "white man who walked a black dog"—the U.S. soldier inciting a black dog against a blindfolded prisoner in the Iraqi jail of Abu Ghraib.[30]

In this way, "A Hard Rain's A-Gonna Fall" becomes a soundtrack for another "warning," the human and environmental disaster that is about to come, that is already here. Later, the song was used as a semi-official anthem for the 2009 Copenhagen Climate Change Conference—quite an ironic homage, in view of the conference's disappointing outcome. It is a fact, however, that today we can recognize that "Hard Rain" is not only about an apocalypse to come but also about an apocalypse in progress. Indeed, it was this way from the beginning: "The pellets of poison *are flooding* their waters"; the waters were already being poisoned, the oceans are already "dead."[31]

At the time we thought it was a metaphor; history has made it literally real. In Taranto, Italy, where a huge steel factory is literally poisoning the town, "wind and rain are synonymous with fear" and "a red-hued river crosses the streets around the harbor near the plant and flows to the sea [in] a stream caused by abundant rain and dust."[32] We need not wait for the hard rain to fall. Other rains, symbols and consequences of a way of life and an economy based on fossil fuels and renewable resources, killing oceans and create "sad" forests: "As acid rain falls on a forest it trickles through the leaves of the trees, runs down into the soil. Some of it finds its way into streams and then into rivers and lakes." "This rain can sting" with "no sign of pain," warns Peter Gabriel; and punk rock's D.R.I.: "Acid rain [is] dissolving away / the monuments of man."[33]

"Hard Rain," indeed, seems to live on in punk music's catastrophic imagination. "Acid rain is up my nose and in my eyes / Poison fish, polluted skies / It makes my flowers die." Bob Rivers's "Acid Rain," written in the rainy city of Seattle, a wry parody of the Beatles' "Penny Lane," replete with black humor and double entendres, is only one of the many pieces in which rap, progressive rock, psychedelic rock, and other contemporary genres recognize acid rain (at times, in conjunction with other "acids") as the metonymy and epitome of the ongoing disaster.[34] Malvina Reynolds's image of the child in the garden in the rain returns as a rain that purifies as it kills, in the Avenged Sevenfold heavy metal sound: "Children still play in the garden," but "not even stars last forever/ Cleanse us, Acid Rain." Acid rain is the new fallout; Minkoff and Hellerman's atomic "Come Away Melinda" is echoed twenty years later by hardcore punk Reagan Youth's "Acid Rain." "Daddy, daddy, can I go out and play? / No son, you'd better stay inside . . . and be safe from acid rain."[35]

Hard rain is already falling. Rivers carry the poison to the sea and kill the oceans "dead." The graves gape open already, the diamond highways are already empty, blood drips from branches that are already broken. The wave that can wipe out, if not the "whole world," at least New York and Amsterdam, Venice and Mumbai, is already mounting, as global warming melts polar ice, swells up the sea, and once more raises the nuclear nightmare. "With climate change many nuclear plants around the world are now threatened by rising waters," Amitav Ghosh writes. "Essential cooling systems could fail; contaminants could seep into the plant and radioactive water could leak out, as happened at the Fukushima Daiichi plant."[36]

Amitav Gosh denounces the blindness of modern literary and cinematic imagination, incapable of narrating the ongoing environmental disaster. Music has done a little better, though songs usually focus less on slow, ongoing processes than on specific catastrophic events—floods, earthquakes, fires, hurricanes, droughts. Such stories are at the very roots of Bob Dylan's poetics, from Woody Guthrie to the blues. Guthrie sang of another "hard" rain, not liquid water but powdery dust that hit the rural Southwest in an apocalytic "dark mysterious storm"; "we could see the dust cloud comin', the cloud looked deathlike black . . . we thought it was our Judgment, we thought it was our doom."[37]

The blues, in turn, memorialized the great Mississippi floods as another end of the world. Charlie Patton's "High Water Everywhere" was one of Bob Dylan's inspirations; "The water was rising up in my friend's door / The man said to his womenfolk, 'Lord we'd better go.'"[38] Or Bessie Smith's *Back Water Blues*," which Bob Dylan sang in concert at Carnegie Hall: "It rained five days and the skies turned dark as night." Two images of apocalypse in one verse: the Flood (as in the classic spiritual, "Didn't It Rain," "it rained forty days and forty nights without stopping")[39] and the Judgment, combined in the image of the darkness in the sky that it shares with Woody Guthrie and other ends-of-the-world, from the Great Depression (The Carter Family, "this dark hour of midnight nearing") to Hurricane Katrina (Tom Morello, "it's midnight in the city of destruction").[40]

"If the levees break again . . ." Tom Morello's warning is a direct quote from another blues song about the 1927 flood, Memphis Minnie's "When the Levee Breaks": "If it keeps on rainin' the levee's gonna break / And the water gonna come in, all of these people have no place to stay." It doesn't take a "hard" rain to make a disaster, an excess of ordinary rain will do.[41] Through Memphis Minnie, however, Tom Morello also refers to Bob Dylan, who pays homage to her in "The Levee's Gonna Break," and to Charlie Patton in "High Water (For Charley Patton)."[42]

The waters were already rising, in another kind of apocalypse and judgment, in *The Times They Are a-Changing'*. Bob Dylan has a fascination of his own with floods. In *The Basement Tapes*, another blues song of the 1927 flood (John Lee Hooker's "Tupelo") shares space with The Band's "Crash on the Levee."[43] The meaning is always the same: the rain is a-gonna fall, the levee is about to break. Yet, Bob Dylan's position across the third millennium line is not the same as that of his sources and inspirations in the twenties and thirties. For Bessie Smith, Memphis Minnie, Charlie Patton, Woody Guthrie, and A. P. Carter, the flood, the dust storm, and the Depression are literal "ends of the world" as described by the Italian ethnologist Ernesto deMartino: the lived experience of apocalypses that submerge their daily reality generating a "loss of presence" that leaves them uprooted and stranded, literally with no direction home.[44] In the Carters' "No Depression in Heaven," "lost millions" are swept "to their doom"; Memphis Minnie, alone after the flood, has "nobody to tell [her] troubles to." It is not just about the loss of home, but rather about the angst of not having a "place to live," the disappearance of objects, sights, and relationships that once made the world recognizable. "Thousands people stands on the hill, looking down where they used to stay / Children stand there screaming, mama, we ain't got no home," Blind Lemon Jefferson sings.[45] Woody Guthrie's dust storm is not "dark" only because it hides the sun, but also because it is "mysterious," incomprehensible—"hard" in another sense, too.

In a different context, anthropologist Vito Teti speaks of "malinconia da catastrofe," and of course "malinconia" (melancholy) is the term most often used in Italian to translate "blues." The loss of cultural and spatial references, Teti comments, generates a sense of displacement "intrinsic to the history and anthropology of individuals faced with the constant danger of a loss of presence."[46] Literal displacement, and its psychological impact, is the theme of many classic disaster blues and songs. Bessie Smith again, in "Back Water Blues":

> It thundered and lightnin'd
> And the wind began to blow
> There was thousands of people
> They had no place to go.

In Woody Guthrie's "The Great Dust Storm," the erasure of recognizable space referents is followed by forced displacement:

It covered up our fences, it covered up our barns
It covered up our tractors in this wild and dusty storm
We loaded our jalopies and piled our families in
We rattled down that highway to never come back again.

For Bob Dylan, on the other hand, these are not lived experiences but the historical memory of other people's tragedies, forewarnings or returns of religious apocalypses, or metaphors for other things. We can read Dylan's end-of-the-world visions in literal religious terms: a prophecy of the biblical Armageddon, as in "Señor (Tales of Yankee Power)," in which case it would be about Dylan's own religious faith. Or we could read them as metaphors, the end of the world and the end of history as the figure of a sense of displacement and loss of presence caused less by specific events than by a broader loss of meaning in the relationships among human beings and between human beings and their world; "This place don't make sense to me no more."[47]

"The Levee's Gonna Break" alternates verses about the flood and verses about a human relationship gone bad. "If it keep on rainin' the levee gonna break / I tried to get you to love me, but I won't repeat that mistake." But, if we hear them in context, even the most literal images of the flood evoke less its material than its moral impact, the collapse is as ethical as it is physical; the levee breaks, and someone will rob you of all they can take, the levee breaks and so many people don't know where to turn. "Can you tell me where we're headin'? / Lincoln County Road or Armageddon?"[48]

"If you go down in the flood / It's gonna be your own fault," Dylan sings with The Band.[49] In the context of the environmental crisis, "Hard Rain" warns us that the rain that is going to fall is not the cause but the consequence and the culmination of a catastrophe that we have brought on ourselves. We are the ones who poisoned both waters and human relationships and created worlds of violence, solitude, and lies. The "pellets of poison," Dylan explained, are "all the lies that people get told on their radios and in their newspapers . . . trying to take people's brains away. Which maybe has been done already."[50] The message here is less in the rather lame reference to mass media than in that ominous "already." It has happened already; it is already happening.

I am thinking of the most cryptic line in "Hard Rain"; in what sense does the "home in valley" meet "the damp dirty prison"? Is it a paradox, the encounter of two opposites, or a fusion, the rural idyll contaminated by the prison nightmare and turning into a nightmare itself? Is the prison already presaged in the home? And what is the "white ladder covered with water"? It may be the mystic ladder in Jacob's vision in Genesis, celebrated by a classic spiritual, on which angels climb up and down between heaven and earth—but the waters of the Flood rise, hide it, cut us off from the rungs of salvation.[51] The cruel rain that's a-gonna fall is a punishment for our sins, as the spiritual warns us—evoked by Bessie Smith, quoted by James Baldwin, mentioned by Bob Dylan—"God gave Noah the rainbow sign / No more water but the fire next time."[52]

There is no "next time" in "A Hard Rain's A-Gonna Fall"; fire and water shall come together, like the tsunami in Fukushima. The biblical prophecy meets the present danger, metaphor meets history, and the divine punishment that began human history meets the punishment that shall put an end to it.

Chapter Four

WHICH WAY HISTORY?

WHAT'S THE NEWS? WHAT'S THE NEWS?

In many Italian versions of "Il Testamento dell'avvelenato," including Carmela Luci's, when the young man comes home and tells his mother that he is "ill to the heart," she wants to know what he had to eat, and then goes on to ask other questions: "on what did she fry it, my dear gentle son? On a brand new skillet . . . how was it served? With a brand new plate . . . how did you eat it? with a brand new fork . . ."

Oral sources, whether in the form of a life story or a traditional ballad, "tell all the truth but tell it slant."[1] As Zygmunt Bauman points out, "Remembered history is the logic which the actors inject into their strivings and which they employ to invest credibility into their hopes"; therefore, the "'materiality' of remembered history" does not rest on "'truth' as understood by conventional historians."[2] Oral sources, as the privileged vehicle of remembered history, whether individually or in shared traditional forms, accentuate the power that Carlo Ginzburg recognizes in all narrative texts of the historical past: "underneath the textual surface and the explicit information they are meant to convey, even against or beyond the narrators' intentions and awareness, the fragments and traces of a deeper truth."[3]

In a seminal essay, Ginzburg suggested that such "traces" may be the basis of an interpretive method in which "marginal and irrelevant details . . . generally considered trivial and unimportant, 'beneath notice,' furnish the key to the highest achievements of human genius" and help reveal the "outlook of a social class, or of a writer, or of an entire society." By means of "low intuition" and "conjectural knowledge" (*sapere indiziario*), Ginzburg explains, we may identify in individual texts the clues of social patterns of culture and behavior.[4] Oral history and folklore share in this form of knowledge; they couch cultural patterns and world views in narrative form, linguistic quirks, errors, silences, or in the almost invisible changes in individual recollection and performance that respond to the impact of history on socially shared cultural artifacts.

The brand-new skillet, plate, and fork is one such significant detail, the material "trace" of a deep-seated relationship to history, change, and time. Though it may seem an insignificant insertion, only good to expand the pleasure of singing and listening, in fact it reinforces and gives tangible form to the ballad's basic conflict between the safe familiar and the dangerous "new." For the popular classes, "the new" did not always mean improvement and progress. Too many times the life of the communities that created and maintained the tradition of the popular ballad was disrupted by the breaking of "the new," embodied in wars, invasions, forced migration, famine, disease, taxes, natural disasters, economic crises, changes that made them feel that they were subjected to forces that they did not control—*subaltern*, indeed, but not serene in their subordination. As Rodney Hilton's study of early peasant rebellions shows, "innovation by the lords" was one cause of revolts in which rebellious peasants saw themselves as defending the "old law" and "tended to cling to custom even when, without knowing, they were constantly seeking to mould custom to suit their interests."[5]

The history of "Lord Randal"/"Il testamento dell'avvelenato" accompanies and illuminates the process of social change that produced modern class society. The popular ballad as a genre flourished in Britain at the time of enclosures and vagrancy laws, when modernization and innovation meant the privatization of the commons that turned many rural proletarians into disciplined factory workers or urban poor and illegal vagrants. Rooted in a traditional world in which "the law drew a sharp dividing line between the relative security of the inherited space [*the home, the bed*] and the terrifying inhospitality of the rest [*the wildwood*]," "Lord Randal" circulates during a transitional time in which the relative security of the familiar was swept away by new pervasive forms of power and control. Bauman's "memory of class" of the old order becomes a tool of resistance and survival in the new.[6]

African American blues and Italian folk and partisan ballads share a revealing incipit: "woke up this morning," "l'altra mattina mi son svegliato." You wake up in the morning and the devil is knocking at your door (Robert Johnson), the blues is walking around your bed (Bessie Smith), the enemy is invading your land ("Bella ciao," Italian partisan song), my baby has left me (B. B. King), my lover is out walking with someone else ("Fior di tomba," Italian folk ballad). The new day brings new threats—evil, invasion, depression, treason, desertion. Folk song, as part of "remembered history," expresses what anthropologist Vito Teti describes as the state of mind of "mobile people" whose experience of natural disasters and sociohistorical disruption make them uncertain and melancholy but also creative and resilient in the struggle against new and old dangers and in the "search for alternative paradises elsewhere."[7]

Mobile people, paradises elsewhere—departures and desertions. Had it not been for departures and desertions, "Il testamento dell'avvelenato" would never have become "Lord Randal," and we would not be able to read "Hard Rain" as also a story of migration. And yet, Lord Randal goes hunting into the wildwood, Dylan's blue-eyed son explores oceans, highways, mountains; both leave their mothers at home, to make their bed and ask questions when—if—they return. To the bold travelers and wanderers who survive to tell the tale, this becomes a story of adventure and achievement, as in many songs of emigration. On the one hand, an Italian folk song I heard on both sides of the Atlantic celebrates the fact that "with our labor, we Italians built cities and towns."[8] On the other hand, however, to those who stay behind migration is a form of betrayal. In a song by Somali migrant poet Geedi Yusuf, a woman who was left at home blames her husband for "trading your homeland and your children for a bottle of wine and a pallet in an Italian street."[9]

Many Italian emigration songs share with "Lord Randal" the theme of generational conflict as historical metaphor. Take the best-known and most popular Italian emigration song, as sung by the great traditional singer Italia Ranaldi, from Poggio Moiano, near Rome:

> Mamma mamma damme cento lire che all'America vojo
> anna'
> Cento lire te le darei, ma all'America no no no
> Il fratello dalla finestra je disse mamma lasciala annà'
> Vanne via fija maledetta in mezzo al mare pozzi restà'
> Quando fu alla metà der mare il bastimento je
> s'affonnò . . . [10]
> (Mama give me 100 lire, I want to go to America
> I'd give you 100 lire, but don't go to America
> Her brother spoke from the window: Mama, let her go
> OK, go, and you'll be cursed, may you die in the middle
> of sea
> When the boat was halfway across the sea it sank
> down . . .)[11]

For those who were left behind, emigration was a loss as final as death: like Dylan's wandering son, the ballad's wayward daughter sinks in the ocean—stricken by her mother's curse, and because she would be lost forever anyway. To the mothers at home, emigration does not sound like a bold move in search of a better life, but like a desertion from the struggle for survival that those who stay carry on. These songs evince the pain and resentment of those who cannot foresee a future of social progress and improvement and feel the loss of all the traditional guarantees that supported their way of life.[12] In this sense, perhaps, "Lord Randal" may also have a meaning in the third millennium, a time in which "the new" takes the form of the class struggle of the top against the bottom, "reform" means erosion of hard-won rights, and social struggles no longer look forward to revolution but only strive to protect and retain what is left of existing social and economic rights (which is why, like the ballad, they are dubbed "conservative").[13]

And yet, there are not only moments of dread in history, but also hope for the future. When it seems that the times might be changing, "the new" may be perceived not as an aggression from above and outside but also as an impulse of liberation from below. In colonized Ireland, the English authorities were afraid that the traditional Irish salutation, "what's the news" (or, in more vernacular form, "what's the craic") was a subversive expression of dissatisfaction with the present state of things, if not an outright announcement of revolt. Take a beloved Irish song of rebellion, "Kelly, The Boy from Killane." Written by Patrick James McCall in 1898 to commemorate the centennial of the Irish rebellion of 1798, this song bridges the memory of a rebellious past with the vision of liberation to come—1798 to 1916, as it were:

> What's the news? What's the news? O my bold
> Shelmalier
> With your long-barrelled gun of the sea?
> Say what wind from the sun blows his messenger here
> With a hymn of the dawn for the free?
> Goodly news, goodly news, do I bring, Youth of Forth.[14]

This process—from the "memory" of a (re)imagined past to the imagination of a possible future can also be traced in the early British songs of the industrial revolution. As Ian Watson notes, early industrial songs reflect the reaction to a "traumatizing industrialization of Britain" imposed from above, which brought about "a worsening of living conditions for a large section of the population." The songs of the working class responded to the "negative effects of 'progress' " by projecting them against a largely mythic pre-industrial Golden Age. As Karl Marx, quoted by Watson, noted in *Capital*, "time and experience were needed" before workers "could come to direct their attacks, not against the material instruments of production, but against the social form in which these instruments are used." In the process, the mythic memory of the past "Golden Age" can evolve into McCall's "hymn of the dawn" or the vision of the rising "sun of the future" (*sol dell'avvenir*), as immortalized in the Italian "Workers' Anthem" (*Inno dei lavoratori*) written in 1886 by Socialist Party founder Filippo Turati, and in the Resistance song "Fischia il vento"—"the wind blows," the song says, and the partisans didn't need a weatherman to tell them which way it blew.[15]

The meaning of "the new," then, changes with the times, between fear and hope, depending on which way the times are changing and who is changing them. There is, however, no apocalypse in the ballad's vision of history: no matter what happens, we will survive. This is what the testament in "Lord Randal" is about. The hero dies, killed by "the new" embodied by the lover; but the testament indicates that his family and community will live on, that someone will survive to receive his symbolic heritage and continue the familiar roles and functions. "Lord Randal" spans the time of the rise of the modern world, the rise and decline of the industrial revolution, as a time of danger but also of survival and struggle. Dylan's "Hard Rain" belongs in a time after Auschwitz and Hiroshima, when the extinction of humankind has become a literal possibility. So, while it also ends with a testament, the poet's prophetic song, it envisions no future, no survivors, no heirlooms. Both "testaments," however, have the same ritual function: elaborating the loss, finding meaning in the meaninglessness of death and disaster, and, as Ernesto de Martino famously phrased it, "turning the loss into value."[16]

THE GARDEN OF FORKING PATHS

It would be a mistake, then, to derive from "Lord Randal" the assumption that folk song and oral cultures are always oriented toward the defensive order of the familiar and the past. Unlike the songs of protest, union, and civil rights that Bob Dylan labels "political," popular ballads do not ask "which side are you on"—sheriff Blair or the National Miners' Union, Bull Connor or Martin Luther King, war or peace . . . Through the centuries, ballads have belonged to people on both "sides"—young and old, women and men—so they are about those conflicts in which taking sides is impossible. Each ballad, or the ballad repertoire as a whole, states a dilemma, but does not resolve it: like in Jorge Luis Borgés's "garden of forking paths,"[17] the story can go either way, because in the ballad, like in classical tragedy, reasons are divided, all sides are both right and fatal—the new is dangerous and threatening, but can we give up the future?

Indeed, if we listen to the ballads and take them seriously as interpretations of history, we may reach a better understanding of Bob Dylan's work. So, what follows is a digression that will ultimately take us back to Bob Dylan anyway. It was not only the young Bob Dylan of the folk revival years, but also the more mature artist at the turn of the century, who was steeped in the logic and poetry of the ballads, as though the folk songs he had learned back then returned decades later as deep-seated patterns of imagination and memory.

Take "Tin Angel," from Dylan's 2012 *Tempest*:

> It was late last night when the boss came home
> To a deserted mansion and a desolate home.

And listen to Woody Guthrie:

> It was late last night when the boss came home
> Askin' for his lady
> The only answer that he got,
> "She's gone with the Gypsy Davey,
> She's gone with the Gypsy Dave."[18]

"The Gypsy Laddie" (Child 200) is one of the best-known ballads in the British and American canon. In England and Scotland, the song is about a lord, in Woody Guthrie and Bob Dylan's America some kind of rancher, but the story is always the same: the home is empty because the lady has left to follow a gypsy or a wanderer and live with him on the road. Once again, the opposition is between the home and the road, the known and the unknown, the old and the new, safety and adventure, family and strangers. Dylan sings this ballad as "Blackjack Davey" on his folk album *Good as I Been to You* (1992), and rewrites it as the first part of "Tin Angel." As in the ballad, the boss mounts his horse (a "milkwhite steed" in Britain, a "buckskin horse" in Woody Guthrie, a "buckskin mare" in Dylan), goes after his wife, finds her, and asks her to return home.

At this point, however, "Tin Angel" grafts parts of another ballad, "Matty Groves": the husband kills his wife's lover (that Dylan names Henry Lee, like the hero in "Love Henry," another tragic ballad), then she kills him, repents, and kills herself (in "Matty Grove" the husband kills the wife and himself). In the end they are all buried in a common grave (echoes of "Barbara Allen"). "Tin Angel," then, is a tapestry of ballads, which in Dylan's hands turn into "a western tale, a gangster story, a chivalric romance, a noir."[19] Appropriately, it ends in a massacre; like in "Hard Rain," there are no survivors.

The ballad is much more complex. The folk variants of "Gypsy Laddie" offer no fixed ending, but rather a question that generates a spate of possible solutions. In their dialogue, the lord tries to persuade his runaway wife to return home, to wealth, safety, loved ones; "O come go home with me my dearie / Come home and be my lover / I'll furnish you with a room so neat / With a silken bed and cover" (Jean Ritchie); "Have you forsaken your house and home / Have you forsaken your baby / Have you forsaken your husband dear / To go with the Gypsy Davy?" (Woody Guthrie). In different variants, the lady's answers are divided, just as divided she herself must be between the home (the baby) or the road (the lover). Sometimes she returns: "O soon this lady changed her mind / Her clothes grew old and faded / Her hose and shoes fell from her feet / And left her bare and naked" (Jean Ritchie). Sometimes, she stays defiantly on the road: "I will leave my house and home / Then gently spoke the lady / I'll ride with the gypsum over the plain / And you can have the baby" (from the Ozarks, collected by Vance Randolph).[20] Neither conclusion, yes or no, is more authoritative or "authentic"; the ballad contradicts itself because it *contains*— includes, recognizes, and understands—multiple possibilities.

The same moral dilemma is at the core of "Cecilia," one of the best-known Italian ballads, whose traces we will also find in Bob Dylan's canon. Cecilia's husband is in jail; she begs the "captain" to release him, and he agrees on condition that she spend a night with him. Cecilia asks her husband what she ought to do, and at this point the ballad forks between diverging paths: how to choose between saving the husband's life or the wife's integrity, between a hanging and a rape? Will the male hero display cynical egotism or selfless generosity? Two versions, recorded at the same time, from a mother and her son, give opposite answers. Gallerana Orsini, from Polino, Umbria, sings "Vacci vacci Cecilia, vacci pure a dormi' / Rivestiti da sposa, sappi ben compari'." ("Go, go, Cecilia, go sleep with him / wear your wedding dress, look the best you can"). And her son, Luigi Matteucci: "Senti cara Cecilia, Cecilia del mio cuore / Riguardati l'amore, Riguardati l'onore / Non ti curar di me" ("Listen, Cecilia of my heart / protect of your love, protect your honor / don't worry about me"). Cecilia chooses to submit to the blackmail, but the "captain" kills her husband anyway and again the ballad proposes alternatives: in some versions, she kills the "captain" in revenge; in others, she retires to a convent.[21]

"The Gypsy Laddie" and "Cecilia" stage the dilemma within a single ballad and its variants. "Lord Randal" instead seems to take only one side, that of the mother, the home, the past; but in this case, the alternative between the different options is established not *within* one ballad but *between* ballads; "Lord Randal" is balanced, among others, by "The Lass of Roch Royal" (Child 76), in which it is the past that kills the future. In "Lord Randal," the male hero goes out to meet his "true love" and is killed; in "The Lass of Roch Royal," the heroine leaves her father's house to join her love, crosses the wild sea with her baby in her arms, but when she knocks at his castle's gate in the chilly wind and the driving rain, his mother turns her back and sends her and her child out to die in the stormy sea. Taken together, "Lord Randal" and "The Lass of Roch Royal" tell us that it is impossible to take sides between continuity and change: the new may tear apart our familiar world, but the old can kill a desirable future. In other words, those who have reasons to fear the future are not necessarily satisfied with the present.

"Lord Randal" is also balanced by another ballad that is known in Southern Italy and throughout the English-speaking world, and also had influences on Bob Dylan: "Il riscatto della bella" (The fair lady's ransom) or "The Maid Freed from the Gallows" (aka "The Pricklie Bush," "Gallows Pole," "Hangman"). In "Lord Randal," a young man is killed by his lover and assisted by his mother; in "The Maid Freed from the Gallows," a young woman is betrayed by her parents and saved by her true love. She is about to die on the gallows for some undefined transgression; she asks her mother, father, and brother to pay her ransom, but they refuse, and she is finally saved when her lover arrives with silver and gold. Once again, there is an Italian antecedent, the Sicilian epic of "Scibilia Nobili," in which the lady is kidnapped by pirates, taken from port to port in search of ransom, and finally saved by her husband.[22] This is how I heard the ballad in 2013 from my friend Maria Adorni, who learned it as a child from her grandmother in Calabria:

> Gira navi e vota navi e la bella piangendo sta
> Portatemi a quello porto dove mia madre sta
> O madre mia carissima riscattami di ccà
> O figlia mia carissima quant'è lo tò riscatto
> Tri barcuni, tri liuni, 'na colonna d'oro ci sta
> È meglio ca ti perdissi che tant'oro mò s'inni va.[23]
> (Round and round goes the ship and the lady weeps
> Take me to the harbor where my mother lives
> Dearest mother, rescue me from here
> Dearest daughter, how much is your ransom
> Three gold coins, three boatloads, a pile of gold
> I'd rather lose you than lose all this gold).

In the English-speaking variants, the pirates are replaced by a judge or a hangman. Julia Scaddon, from Chideock, Dorset, in the fifties:

> O hangman, hold my hand
> and hold it for a while

I think I see my own mother dear
Comin' over the yonder style.
Oh have you brought me gold?
Or can you set me free?
Or are you come to see me hang
All on the gallows tree?[24]

Walter Lucas, as recorded by Peter Kennedy in 1951 at Sixpenny Handley, Dorset:

O I've no gold
Or silver to set you free
For I am come for to see you
Alone on the gallows tree.

Only the "lover" or the "sweetheart dear" arrives in the nick of time with gold and silver to save the maid from the gallows:

Yes I've brought gold
And silver to pay your fee
For to keep your body from the cold clay ground
And your neck from the gallows tree.[25]

On the brink of death, the maid also stands on the edge of time. Once again, the contrast between generations functions as a metaphor for the contrast between the old and the new, the past and the future. This may be why the ballad is especially popular in the future-oriented United States, where it also enters the African American tradition, as a *cante-fable* in the repertoire of Huddie Ledbetter, or as a story about the 1965 rebellion in Los Angeles in which a young looter obtains from his social worker the bail money denied by his parents.[26]

In this way, the ballad tradition deals with the dramatic tension between the familiar and the new, continuity and change. There is, however, another turn of the screw. In Led Zeppelin's hard-rock version (based on Huddie Ledbetter's), "Gallows Pole," the story is complicated further. In the first place, there are no father and mother, only brother and sister; in rock counterculture, old generations are irrelevant or non-existent, while solidarity, rather than conflict, prevails among "brothers" and "sisters" (not necessarily by blood). Both come forward to save the young man from the gallows: the brother brings gold, the sister gives her body. In the absence of parental figures, however, the old still wield their evil power: the hangman takes the gold, rapes the woman, and kills his victim.

> Oh, yes, you got a fine sister,
> She warmed my blood from cold,
> Brought my blood to boiling hot
> To keep you from the Gallows Pole,
> Your brother brought me silver,
> Your sister warmed my soul,
> But now I laugh and pull so hard
> And see you swinging on the Gallows Pole.[27]

By introducing the hangman's sexual blackmail and his final betrayal, Led Zeppelin connect "Gallows Pole" also to the story of "Cecilia." Now, "Cecilia" does not exist in ballad form in the

English-speaking world, though (with a tacked-on happy ending) it has an equivalent in William Shakespeare's *Measure for
Measure* (also derived from an Italian source).[28] There are, however, parallels in the singer-songwriter tradition. In "Anathea,"
written by Lydia Wood and Neil Rock and recorded by Judy
Collins and Odetta (based on a Hungarian ballad related to
"Cecilia"), a young man is about to be hanged for stealing a
horse; his sister tries to save him and, against his will, accedes to
the judge's request, and is betrayed:

> Anathea did not heed him
> Straight way to the judge went running
> In his righteous arms at midnight
> There she heard the gallows groaning.[29]

Bob Dylan's version brings it all back home. His song "Seven
Curses" is a synthesis of all the threads we have been following
so far: the request of a ransom, as in "The Maid Freed from the
Gallows"; the sexual blackmail and betrayal, as in "Cecilia"; the
young woman as attempted savior and the nocturnal landscape,
as in Led Zeppelin and "Anathea."

> When the judge he saw Reilly's daughter
> His old eyes deepened in his head,
> Sayin', "Gold will never free your father,
> The price, my dear, is you instead."
>   "Oh I'm as good as dead," cried Reilly,
>   "It's only you that he does crave
>   And my skin will surely crawl if he touches you at all.

Get on your horse and ride away"
Oh father you will surely die
If I don't take the chance to try
And pay the price and not take your advice
For that reason I will have to stay
  The gallows shadows shook the evening
  In the night a hound dog bayed
  In the night the grounds were groanin'
  In the night the price was paid.[30]

Dylan, however, changes a crucial detail. Unlike a brother and sister as in "Anathea" or a daughter rejected by her parents as in "The Maid Freed from the Gallows," in Dylan's "Seven Curses," the person who is about to be hanged is a father, and the one who tries to save him is his daughter. Once again, Dylan illuminates the meaning of his story by adding a word that is not to be found in any of his sources: the daughter tries to save "*old* Riley" but is coveted by the judge's "*old* eyes" and finally betrayed. In this way, Dylan reinstates and complicates the ballad's generational conflict as a metaphor for history: will the young save the old, or will the old again betray them?

In true ballad style, young Dylan leaves the dilemma open. A generation later, however, he is more pessimistic—or realistic. As Alessandro Carrera notes, in the late 1980s he again began to include in his concert playlists folk ballads like "Barbara Allen" or "Golden Vanity." In concert, he prefaced "Golden Vanity" by saying that this song is about everything that is going on today, "and more"; Carrera, however, wonders, "What does 'Golden Vanity,' an English ballad about a heroic young sailor betrayed by his captain, have to do with 'what is going on today'?" He then concludes, "Nothing, not anymore."[31] I would not be so sure. Let us listen to the ballad. This is how Dylan performed it at concert at Waikiki, Hawaii, on April 24, 1992:

> There was a little ship
> And it sailed along the sea
> And the name of that ship was the Golden Vanity
> And she sailed in the low and lonesome ocean
> And she sailed in the lonesome sea.
>> There was another ship sailing along the sea
>> and the name of that ship was the Turkish Revelry
>> and sailing down that low and lonesome ocean
>> sailing in the lonesome sea.

A young cabin boy volunteers to swim to the enemy ship, drill a hole "with his brace and auger in her side," and sink it. The captain promises him gold, land, and his daughter's hand. He succeeds, sinks the ship, swims back—and at this point, as always, the versions of the ballad part ways. In some (e.g., Child's A text), his mates pull him back on board and all ends happily. Most often, however, the captain reneges on his promise and leaves him to drown in the sea. Here, the path forks again: will the young man die alone, or will he take revenge and sink the others with him? Sometimes (as in Pete Seeger's version), he drills a hole in the side of the Golden Vanity and sinks it along with its unfaithful captain and hapless crew. Sometimes, instead, as in the version chosen by Bob Dylan, he chooses a lonesome death:

If it wasn't for the love that I have onto your men
I would do onto you like I done onto them
I'd sink you in the low and lonesome ocean
Sink you in that lonesome sea
So he bowed his breath and down went he.

The song may not be about "all things," but it does evoke
themes that are crucial to Dylan's work, from "Seven Curses"
to "Masters of War" to "The Times They Are A-Changin' ": the
young save, the old betray. Only, now "Things Have Changed":
there is no salvation in sight, the power of the old kills the
future, history's only direction is toward the abyss. The young
cabin boy is abandoned on the ocean, perhaps the same waters
on which the blue-eyed boy stands at the end of his journey;
and, like him, he can only send a last unheard message of solidarity and love before he starts sinking.

CROSSROADS

In "A Hard Rain's A-Gonna Fall," the rain is about to fall and
there is nothing we can do about it. Bob Dylan's vision of the
future is even gloomier than in "Lord Randal": the hero's testament suggests no hope of continuity and survival, only the
prophecy of rain that is to fall, that perhaps is already falling.

Dylan is part of an American countercultural tradition that
never believed that technological improvement and social and
human progress were inseparable, and indeed often suspected
that the opposite was true: "I got into the driver's seat / And I

drove down 42nd Street / In my Cadillac / Good car to drive after a war" ("Talkin' World War III Blues"). A dark vision of the future and a sense of inevitable death run through "Talkin' World War III Blues," "Let Me Die in My Footsteps," or "Masters of War": "the worst fear that can ever be hurled" is "fear to bring children into the world."

What makes "Masters of War" different from all the anti-war songs of its time is the open acknowledgment of hatred in the last line and the absence of any vision of victory over the masters of war. There is no hope for any positive, collective action. In this song, as in "Hard Rain," the hero is alone and helpless; he can only hope to outlive the masters of war so he can sit on their grave in an apocalyptic pale afternoon.[32]

However, "Masters of War" and "Hard Rain" do not stand alone in the early Bob Dylan canon. Like the traditional ballad genre, Dylan was also able to contain opposite ideas in his mind at the same time. "The wind of destruction . . . blows in 'A Hard Rain's A-Gonna Fall'; the wind of change blows in 'The Times They Are A-Changin'."[33] The winds of change, the rising waters of liberation, stood for the irresistible revolt of the young versus the old:

Come gather 'round people wherever you roam
And admit that the waters around you have grown
And accept it that soon you'll be drenched to the bone
If your time to you is worth savin'
Then you better start swimmin' or you'll sink like a stone
For the times they are a-changin'.

Bob Dylan composed "The Times They Are a-Changin' " in the same year in which he recorded "Had Rain" and "Masters of War." At some point in his life, then, Dylan stood at the cross-roads of despair or hope, apocalypse or liberation, and looked both ways to see which way the wind was blowing, whether the rain was falling or the sea was rising. Later, he would decide that he needed no weatherman and went his own way. But he did have that crossroads moment between two imagined futures—and we remember.

Alessandro Carrera was absolutely right when he wrote that Bob Dylan's later albums (but I would say all of his work) are "perhaps the last modernist poem in American litera-ture."[34] Now, twentieth-century modernism has a problem-atic relationship with history. For most of the great modernist writers of the past century, history is a "wasteland" (a "deso-lation row"?) of decadence and defeat, the worldly sequel to the biblical Fall. Many of the great modernists—T.S. Eliot, William Butler Yeats, Joseph Conrad, William Faulkner, Ezra Pound, Jorge Luis Borgés, Luigi Pirandello—had no faith in progress; if anything, they were ideologically conser-vative or frankly reactionary. Yet they are great not *in spite of* their ideology, but precisely *because* of it: their pessimistic view of history and humankind generates an uncompromising metapolitical critique to the state of things, to received ideas and myths, a pitiless unmasking of the logic and the icons of worldly power ("Even the President of the United States sometimes must have to stand naked").[35] It is no wonder that the political Right does not love or understand them, and that it was the young anti-fascists who identified in them the *pars destruens* of a revolutionary vision of change, and carried their books when they went to fight for democracy in Spain. The modernist critique of history can be self-absolutory; there is nothing we can do, so there is nothing we ought to do, it is not our fault, and our only responsibility lies in being part of the human race. But it can be, as in most cases is, utterly radical; power is smooth, solid, offers no contradictions for us to seize and overturn it. There is no way out other than death or the apocalypse.

Joan Baez said once that Bob Dylan "criticizes society, and I criticize it, but he ends up saying that there is not a goddamned thing you can do about it, so screw it. And I say just the opposite."[36] She was wrong. Even in his darkest moments, Dylan is never cynical, and anyway, "doing something about it" is not what he has been about. The task he has taken upon himself is to make us aware of where we stand in the "desolation row" in which we live.[37] Whether we just give up or take up arms to escape or to fight it is our decision, not his. If the wasteland is a "lonesome valley" or a "low and lonesome sea," we cannot expect Bob Dylan, or anyone else, to cross it for us.

However—to end on a personal note in this deeply personal book—if a future apocalypse were to wipe out all of Bob Dylan's songs and we could only save one, I would take with me the one that, for half a century and more, every time I listen—and listen again and again and again—has filled me with a stormy brew of passion for an imagined future, pain for a future lost, and the urge to keep on searching. The song is on *The Times They Are A-Changin'*, and its title is "When the Ship Comes In."

Oh the time will come up
When the winds will stop
And the breeze will cease to be breathin'
Like the stillness in the wind
'Fore the hurricane begins
The hour when the ship comes in.

Time *will* come, not if the ship comes in, but when. Like "Hangman" upends and balances "Lord Randal," the prophecy in "When the Ship Comes In" subverts and balances "Hard Rain." We stand at that prodigious moment in time when the rain is about to fall, but it is not the end of the world; it is a new wonderful new era, an advent of liberation that parts the waters and shakes the sands and confounds the enemies and the false prophets of doom. Lately, I've begun to associate this image with another ship: the rescue ship *Sea Watch* that defied the Italian government's criminal ban on immigration and broke into the harbor with her precious cargo of refugees saved from the sea.[38]

"When the Ship Comes In" was partly inspired by Bertolt Brecht and Kurt Weill's "Pirate Jenny" (*Seeräuberjenny*), from the *Threepenny Opera*, which Dylan saw in 1962. The textual analogies are clear; the tone, however, is different. "Pirate Jenny" is a dark fantasy of revenge ending in massacre; "When the Ship Comes In" is the shining prophecy of a new era in which the enemy will be defeated, submerged by history. In "Pirate Jenny," the pirate ship "turns around in the harbor shooting guns from her bow," and "on it is me"; in Dylan's song, from the bow not "me," but "we" will announce from the bow the coming of the new world.[39]

At first, in fact, it seems that all we need to do is wait for the ship's messianic arrival. But it is not so. Jolted from their irresponsible slumber, our enemies shall come forward with their hands raised in surrender, shouting "we'll meet all your demands." But it will be too late. When the ship comes in, the time of compromise, of mediation, of concession is over, and "we'll shout from the bow: your days are numbered." *We'll* shout. The ship is not some miraculous deus ex machina coming to save us: *we* are on board, *we*, together, are our own salvation.

> And like Pharaoh's tribe
> They'll be drownded in the tide
> And like Goliath they'll be conquered.

The song is steeped in biblical imagery, but "the chains of the sea" that "have busted in the night" also evoke another, "sacred" text, about a time in which we "have nothing to lose but [our] chains" and "have a world to win."[40] Introducing the song in concert, Dylan once said: "I wanna sing one song, here, recognizing that there are Goliaths here nowadays, and people don't realize who the Goliaths are."[41] Nevio Brunori, a worker and union activist at the ThyssenKrupp steel works in Terni, told me once, at the end of a dramatic cycle of struggle and strikes, "History had taught me that at least one time David managed to defeat Goliath. But then we had to fight two, three, four Goliaths, and they were too many for poor David."[42] And Dylan: "But in the olden days Goliath was slain and everybody now they look back and say how cruel Goliath was. Nowadays we've got crueler Goliaths who do crueler and crueler things, but one day they're gonna be slain, too." Maybe not. But history is not over yet.

Appendix

HISTORY'S LESSONS UNLEARNED

ON MARCH 27, 2020, at the height of the Covid-19 epidemic, Bob Dylan released a sixteen-minute ballad on the assassination of John F. Kennedy that he had composed and recorded at some unspecified time before but never released. This release was followed on April 16, 2020, by another piece, "I Contain Multitudes."[1]

"Murder Most Foul" is another apocalypse of sorts: a lament for the death of John F. Kennedy and the America he represented, and a search into the meaning and uses of history and memory. As always, Bob Dylan is guided by the sound of music and the sound of language: the obsessive repetition of a deceptively simple, deep musical phrase, and the chain of alliteration, rhyme, and anaphora, often leading into surprising and revealing connections between apparently disparate elements. The piece teems with intertextual references and allusions to cultural memory that will keep Dylanologists and exegetes busy for a lifetime.[2] The story it tells is one of death, fall, mourning, and pain that explains much about our times, and Dylan's own trajectory. Here, I can only attempt the beginnings of a temporary, fragile, and fragmentary interpretive path, my own among many possible ones.

Dylan's Kennedy is more of a universal symbol than the tangible, imperfect human being that we knew; hence, his assassination is more than a run-of-the-mill political murder. "They blew off his head," "they blew out the brains of the king." Since the revolutionary birth of the nation, American imagination has been haunted by the symbol of the beheading of the king; revolution on the one hand (ghosts of Cromwell's England), and on the other, the loss of a center, of a reference, of an authority, the vanishing of meaning and order, the absence of a father.[3] It is no wonder that Dylan's piece hinges on a quote from *Hamlet*, the story of a king's murder and the loss of a father. Dylan also evokes *Macbeth*, another regicide, and alludes ("a good day to die") to Crazy Horse, another murdered leader of a people.

As in a lysergic hallucination, Dylan projects the scene of the crime as a "human sacrifice" in which—as in archaic hunting rituals—the killers attempt to possess the victim's power by dismembering his body and appropriating his mind and soul: "They mutilated his body and took out his brain . . . But his soul was not there where it was supposed to be at."[4] Since that day, the soul has not been found again: "the soul of a nation been torn away." Perhaps it may be hiding somewhere waiting to return like the mythological buried king,[5] perhaps it was already dead. Like the sovereigns of myth, Kennedy holds in himself the fate of his land. His death is like *Le Mort d'Arthur* in the chivalric epic—in fact, wasn't the Kennedy circle known as a modern-day "Camelot"?

How does the land respond to the death of her king? "Hush li'l children, you'll soon understand / The Beatles are coming they're gonna hold your hand." The tragedy doesn't teach America to grow up. Like a playful child afraid of the dark—"Slide down the banister, get your coat"—the country takes refuge in the illusion of permanent adolescence. Darkness, however, lurks on the edge of "Aquarian Age" euphoria: the peace and love of Woodstock will soon turn into the blood and violence of Altamont, just like the "home in the valley meets the damp dirty prison" in "Hard Rain"—or perhaps turns into it, or was *contained* by it all the time, like in a Lovecraft tale. "I contain multitudes," Dylan proclaims, quoting Walt Whitman, in his April 2020 release. "Contain" may mean—as in Whitman and possibly Dylan—an inclusiveness that can accommodate contradiction; but it can also mean (as in Don DeLillo's *Underworld*)[6] the containment of a danger pushing to burst out from underneath a veneer of tranquility and peace.

Perhaps, this danger, the sweeping of tragedy under the carpet of adolescence, is part of the reason why Dylan no longer felt part of that time. He could no longer be contained in the Kennedy-era folk revival, but he also opted out of Woodstock's "peace and love." He, too, was lost, with no direction home: a "blackface singer" or a "white face clown," as in the minstrel-show tradition with which he connects in *"Love and Theft,"* or in the mask he wore in the *Rolling Thunder Revue*, adrift in America of disguises, deceit, and whited sepulchers, searching for his own face through decades of restless change.[7]

Forget the Aquarian Age: "The age of the anti-Christ has just only begun." The theological virtues of "Faith, Hope and Charity died," truth is hidden and lost, there is no difference between "[Vietcong] Charlie" and Uncle Sam,[8] and we greet the news with a variation on Rhett Butler's immortal words: "Frankly, Miss Scarlet, I don't give a damn." Yet, in this part of the song, Dylan begins to evoke another side of reality. "We are living in a nightmare on Elm Street" he sings: a Wes Craven horror movie, but also the street where Kennedy was killed, and Deep Ellum to Black bluesmen, as he reminds us in the next line. Elm Street contains Deep Ellum as the b(l)ack side of Dallas, the dangerous red-light district haunted by Ralph Ellison's (or is it H. G. Wells's?) invisible man, the dark face of that sunny November day, the nightmare that Malcolm X saw where Martin Luther King (a symbol of the Kennedy era) saw a dream.

In the third section, Dylan plunges into an exploration of personal and cultural memory, searching perhaps for the runaway soul of the country, and his own. It may be a historical America in which the vision of liberation from slavery in the old spiritual ("Freedom, oh freedom") evolves into the "freedom from want" of Roosevelt's New Deal.[9] Or it may be the America of his adolescence, the radio days of his musical roots: Little Richard's rock and roll, the Everly Brothers' rockabilly, Patsy Cline's country music, the Kingston Trio's folk revival, Louis Armstrong's St. James infirmary—the America of Elvis Presley, another dead king, sexy ("One Night of Sin") and arcane ("Mystery Train"), and of its purest dead queen of beauty and innocence, Marilyn Monroe.

But these adolescent Cold War memories also have an underside of danger. The Everlys' Little Susie slept unconscious through it all. Little Richard's Miss Lizzy was dizzy, Patsy Cline 's great hit was "Crazy"; like Kennedy, Patsy Cline died tragically in 1963, Tom Dooley died on the gallows, whitened cadavers lay in St. James infirmary, Marilyn Monroe and Elvis Presley overdosed. Further back, the work of the New Deal was finished by the war. In a brilliant display of his method of composition, Dylan follows the sound and surfs signifiers to discover unexpected connections among the signifieds: the funny men of our childhood movies— Harold *Lloyd*, Buster Keaton, Bugsy Siegel—flow into the outlaw Pretty Boy *Floyd* (who, in another contradictory turn of the screw, sends us back to Dylan's inspiration, Woody Guthrie). This is, indeed, how memory works: spontaneous associations that reveal unforeseen meanings in shards of experience. A few weeks later, another Floyd was to become the mobilizing symbol of our time.

So Dylan keeps searching. Once again, just as he turned to the blues tradition to renew his creativity in the 1990s, Dylan turns to Black consciousness in search of his country's soul— from downtown Dallas to Deep Ellum, as it were. Like Hamlet's Denmark, America is out of joint and, once again, it may be up to the descendants of the slaves to set it right. As the ballad draws to an end, Black voices gradually emerge and prevail— Charlie Parker and Miles Davis, Nat King Cole and Little Richard, Ella Fitzgerald and Jelly Roll Morton, Etta James and Nina Simone. There are other voices and other references (The Who, Eagles, Beach Boys, Allman Brothers, Randy Newman), but these are the ones that set the tone: after all, they all stand on the shoulders of the Black tradition.

I don't know whether Dylan ever heard one of the spirituals that the anthropologist Bruce Jackson recorded in the sixties at a Texas prison farm.[10] Improvising antiphonally over a tight tapestry of gospel harmony, the leader begins:

> I wanna tell you about a day, children, wasn't it so sad
> I wanna tell you about November 22, wasn't it sad
> I wanna tell you a long time ago children, wasn't it sad
> When they pushed him on up the hill
> They pushed the man on up the hill
> I wanna tell you about a day you will never forget
> The man was riding down the street
> Ridin' down the street in a long black car
> Oh wasn't it sad, Lord, Lord, Lord.

And then another voice takes over:

> One more thing I wanna tell you now children
> I wanna tell you about the woman who was on her dying
>   bed one day
> The same day that they assassinated the president I
>   believe it was . . .

When they hear the news of the President's death, "little children began runnin' and cryin' "; when they realize their mother is dying, her children mourn—"who's gonna wake me up in the morning? who's gonna feed me in the morning?" In the Black consciousness, the murder of Christ, the murder of Kennedy, and the "lonesome death" of a poor Black woman are the same death, and they leave us equally orphaned, like the Aquarium generation after the death of their King. Ishmael's "royal mantle of humanity" falls equally on the shoulders of all.[11] Every murder is foul (*Murder Most Foul* is also an Agatha Christie novel); a king's death stands for every death. In a way, the Texas spiritual is the other side of Dylan's elegy: the president represents all not because he is a king, but because, like Jesus Christ and like Hattie Carroll, he is human.

"When will they ever learn? When will we ever learn?" asks Pete Seeger in a classic song.[12] In the last lines of "Murder Most Foul," Dylan returns, in his own ambiguous and cryptic way, to another tragedy whose lesson America has learned only imperfectly, if at all: the Civil War. He had already evoked it indirectly in his play on Rhett Butler's final words; now, his last request to Wolfman Jack includes "Marching through Georgia" and "The Blood-Stained Banner": the North's victory song and the South's song of defeat, torn by war, unified by blood, death, and destruction. Perhaps, on that November day in 1963 and again in the death-ridden spring of 2020, the blood-stained banner may be the symbol of a defeated and wounded nation (and world) that has a lesson to learn but, like Dylan's Mister Jones, may never know what it is.

NOTES

INTRODUCTION: MEMORY, VOICE, AND THE GLOBAL BOB DYLAN

1. Greil Marcus, *Like a Rolling Stone: Bob Dylan at the Crossroads* (London: Faber and Faber, 2005), 1.
2. The Kingston Trio's hit version of "Tom Dooley" (1958) is on *The Kingston Trio* (Capitol, 1990). The group learned it originally from a recording of the North Carolina traditional singer Frank Proffitt, collected by Frank Warner in 1938. See Frank Proffitt, *North Carolina Songs and Ballads* (Legacy, 1962).
3. Bob Dylan: "I liked the Kingston Trio. Even though their style was polished and collegiate, I liked most of their stuff anyway." *Chronicles: Volume 1* (2004; London, Sydney, New York: Pocket Books, 2005), 32–33.
4. *The Limeliters* (Elektra, 1960).
5. Peter, Paul and Mary, *In the Wind* (Warner Brothers, 1963). On August 28, 1963, the trio sang "Blowin' in the Wind" on the March on Washington stage from which Martin Luther King gave his "I Have a Dream" speech and Bob Dylan sang "Only a Pawn in their Game."
6. *The Best of Joan Baez*, with Bill Wood and Ted Alevizos (*Veritas*, 1959; reissued on CD as *Folksingers 'round Harvard Square*, Hallmark, 1972).

7. "Only a Pawn in Their Game" (1963), from *The Times They Are A-Changin'* (Columbia Records, 1964), is the story of the murder of Medgar Evers, a leader of the National Association for the Advancement of Colored People in Mississippi, killed in 1963 by Byron De La Beckwith, a member of the White Citizens' Council. Beckwith was acquitted twice before he was finally sentenced to life in prison as late as 1994. I didn't know who Medgar Evers was; I learned about him from Bob Dylan. I quote Bob Dylan's lyrics as reported in his books *Lyrics 1961–1968, Lyrics 1969–1982,* and *Lyrics 1983–2012,* ed. Alessandro Carrera (Milan: Feltrinelli, 2016–2017). I use the Italian edition because I will occasionally refer to Carrera's editorial notes and comments. For each song, I give the copyright date as it appears in *Lyrics* and, if other, the date of the album on which it is included. Unless otherwise noted, Bob Dylan albums are all published by Columbia Records.

8. Giovanna Daffini was a former rice field hand and street singer who became a protagonist of the Italian folk music revival. Her recording debut can be heard on *Bella Ciao* (Dischi del Sole, 1965), the live recording of a historic concert of the Nuovo Canzoniere Italiano at the Spoleto Festival of Two Worlds. The unconventional sounds of the folk songs and their antiwar message shocked the festival's elegant audience and caused the organizers to be indicted for "contempt of the Armed Forces." See Giuseppe Morandi, *Spoleto 1964 Bella Ciao Il Diario* (Florence: Istituto Ernesto de Martino, 2012).

9. Bob Dylan had a similar moment, too. "A Woody Guthrie set of about twelve double sided 78 records. I put one on the turntable and when the needle dropped, I was stunned—I didn't know if I was stoned or straight." Dylan, *Chronicles,* 243. I wrote my dissertation in American literature on Woody Guthrie, and it was later published—the first full-length critical study of Woody Guthrie anywhere: *La rivoluzione musicale di Woody Guthrie* (Bari, Italy: De Donato, 1973).

10. It is told in the introduction to *The Death of Luigi Trastulli and Other Stories: Form and Meaning in Oral History* (Albany: State University of New York Press, 1991).

11. Woody Guthrie, quoted in the booklet accompanying the record *Bound for Glory: The Songs and Stories of Woody Guthrie Sung by Woody Guthrie and Told by Will Geer,* ed. Millard Lampell (Folkways, 1961).

12. Bob Dylan's " 'unacceptable' nasal voice . . . amounted to a challenge," like "the keening of a tool being sharpened. For all the singer's humor

and apparent ease, it was the sound of anger." Daniel Wolff, *Grown-up Anger: The Connected Mysteries of Bob Dylan, Woody Guthrie, and the Calumet Massacre* (New York: Harper, 2017), 5, 4. See also Alessandro Carrera, *La voce di Bob Dylan: Una spiegazione dell'America* (Milan: Feltrinelli, 2011), a passionate and convincing interpretation of Bob Dylan's later voice.

13. Interview with Terry Hilton (b. 1953), Newcastle, England, January 10, 2018 (transcript slightly edited for readability). Terry Hilton works for Living History—North East, an oral history center in Sunderland.

14. A slang term originally meaning "whore."

15. On "primary" and "secondary" orality, see Walter J. Ong, *The Presence of the Word: Some Prolegomena for Cultural and Religious History* (New Haven, CT: Yale University Press, 1967).

16. Cesare Bermani, "Canti popolari e storie di vita" in *Storia orale e storie di vita*, ed. Liliana Lanzardo (Rome: Franco Angeli, 1989), 91–118; Gianni Bosio, *L'intellettuale rovesciato* (Milan: Istituto Ernesto de Martino/Jaca Book, 1998), 71–110, 289–96, and passim; Alberto Cirese, *Culture egemoniche e culture subalterne* (Palermo, Italy: Palumbo, 1971); Roberto Leydi, *Il folk music revival* (Palermo, Italy: Flaccovio, 1972); Cesare Bermani, "Guerra guerra ai palazzi e alle chiese . . ." *Saggi sul canto sociale* (Rome: Odradek, 2003). On folk music and history, also see my essays "Typology of Industrial Folk Song," in *The Death of Luigi Trastulli*, 161–93, and "Notes on the anti-Fascist Singing Tradition (1922–2011)," in *The Concept of Resistance in Italy: Multidisciplinary Perspectives*, ed. Laura Mosco and Pietro Pirani (London-New York: Rowman & Littlefield, 2017), 171–91.

17. See my *Biography of an Industrial Town* (New York: Palgrave, 2014) and *They Say in Harlan County: An Oral History* (New York: Oxford University Press, 2011). Dante Bartolini, "Il vile Tanturi" and "Non ti ricordi mamma quella notte" are on the CDs accompanying Alessandro Portelli and Antonio Parisella, *Ribelle e mai domata: Canti e racconti di antifascismo e Resistenza* (Rome: Squilibri, 2014), CD 2, tr. 7 and 16. "Il 17 marzo," covered by Terni working-class folk singer Lucilla Galeazzi, is on her CD *Amore e acciaio* (Zone di Musica, 2005).

18. Jacopo Tomatis, *Storia culturale della canzone italiana* (Milan: Feltrinelli, 2019); Alessandro Portelli, *Bruce Springsteen's America: A Dream Deferred* (Newcastle upon Tyne, UK: Cambridge Scholars, 2019); Alessandro Portelli, *The Text and the Voice: Writing, Speaking and Democracy in American Literature* (New York: Columbia University Press, 1994).

19. Eva Guillorel, David Hopkins, and William G. Pooley, eds., *Rhythms of Revolt: European Traditions and Memories of Conflict in Oral Culture* (London: Routledge, 2018); on the reliability of folklore and folk song as a record of specific events, see Richard Dorson, *American Folklore and the Historian* (Chicago-London: University of Chicago Press, 1971), or the section on "Evaluating Oral Materials" in *Interpreting Local Culture and History*, ed. J. Sanford Rikoon and Judith Austin (Boise and Moscow: Idaho State Historical Society-University of Idaho Press, 1991), 91–144.

20. Woody Guthrie, "Los Angeles New Year's Flood," on *Library of Congress Recordings* (1964; Rounder Records, 1988).

21. The story is mentioned in the liner notes to Bob Dylan's album *The Freewheelin' Bob Dylan* (1963). It is repeated often in Italy, but I have never met anyone who has claimed to have actually been there. The story is that Dylan was also in Italy to be with his then-girlfriend Suze Rotolo, who was studying art at the Università per Stranieri (University for Foreigners) in Perugia, and it was there that they parted ways. Typically, the local narrative has it that "Bob Dylan lost his love" in Perugia because "Suze Rotolo, his Muse and inspiration, chose instead Enzo Bartoccioli, the pride of the Borgo d'Oro [neighborhood], a worker at Perugina" chocolate factory. Sandro Francesco Allegrini, "Quando Bob Dylan a Perugia perse l'amore," *Perugia Today*, October 18, 2019, https://www.perugiatoday.it/attualita/quando-bob-dylan-a-perugia-perse-l-amore.html, retrieved May 2, 2021. According to this unconfirmed story, Dylan went back to Perugia and actually performed there. According to Suze Rotolo's memoir—*A Freewheelin' Time: A Memory of Greenwich Village in the Sixties* (New York: Broadway Books, 2008)—Dylan went to Italy only after she had left, and they were reunited after their return. Rotolo did marry Enzo Bartoccioli in 1972. Her memoir is dedicated to him.

22. Interviews with Rudi Assuntino, Rome, November 28, 2017 and December 16, 2019. Rudi Assuntino's "L'uomo che sa" is on his 33 EP *Uccidi e capirai* (Dischi del Sole, 1965). Rudi Assuntino wrote Italian versions of other American anti-nuclear songs, such as Ann and Marty Cleary's "Strontium 90" and Barry McGuire's "Eve of Destruction." He also wrote a post-nuclear disaster song that he says was inspired by "A Hard Rain's A-Gonna Fall" but sounds more like Dylan's "Talkin' World War III Blues." "Blowin' in the Wind" (1962) is on *The Freewheelin' Bob Dylan*.

23. *Folk Songs* (Parma, Italy: Guanda, 1966).

24. Edoardo Bennato's "Era solo un sogno" and "Le ombre" can be heard (much to my embarrassment) on YouTube, https://www.youtube.com /watch?v=ALo28b272hE retrieved January 8, 2020.

25. Interview with Francesco De Gregori, Rome, December 19, 2017. His album of translated Dylan songs is *De Gregori canta Dylan* (Sony, 2015). Dylan translations exist in many languages, another proof of his global presence. One of my favorites is the Spanish activist and folk singer Toli Morilla's CD, *Diez cantares de Bob Dylan nasturianu. Ten Bob Dylan Songs in the Asturian Language* (Santi Gral, Oviedo, Spain, 2009).

26. Interview with Silvia Baraldini, Rome, November 27, 2017. On *Nashville Skyline* (1969), see Lavinia Greeenlaw, "Big Brass Bed: Bob Dylan and Delay," in *Do You, Mr Jones? Bob Dylan with the Poets & Professors*, ed. Neil Corcoran (London: Vintage, 2017), 71–79.

27. Alessandro Carrera, *Bob Dylan* (Milan: Doppiozero, 2015), kindle edition, loc. 89.

28. Marco Rossari, *Bob Dylan: Il fantasma dell'elettricità* (Turin: Add Editore, 2017). Alessandro Robecchi's latest novel is *Flora* (Palermo, Italy: Sellerio, 2021).

29. Interview with Gaia Resta (1979), Rome, January 17, 2020.

30. "It Ain't Me Babe," on *Another Side of Bob Dylan* (1964).

31. "Maggie's Farm," on *Highway 61 Revisited* (1965).

32. "Restless Farewell," on *The Times They Are A-Changin'* (1964).

33. "All I Really Want to Do," on *Another Side of Bob Dylan*.

34. Bruce Springsteen, "Brilliant Disguise," from *Tunnel of Love* (Sony, 1987). Alessandro Carrera notes: "At least since *Time Out of Mind* (1997), even when he says 'I' it does not seem as if he were speaking of himself, because in fact he is gathering together fragments from all the lyrical tradition of folk, country and blues music, as well as echoes of the epic-lyrical American poetry of the nineteenth century, especially about the Civil War." Carrera, "Il mio viaggio nel labirinto Bob Dylan," https://8thofmay .wordpress.com/2017/05/13/alessandro-carrera-il-mio-viaggio-nel -labirinto-bob-dylan/, retrieved December 23, 2019. Translation mine.

35. Greil Marcus, "Stories of a 'bad song'," *Threepenny Review* 104 (Winter 2006): 6–7. For more testimony on Dylan's sincerity and/or opportunism at the time, see Anthony Scaduto, *Bob Dylan* (New York: Grosset & Dunlap, 1971), 120–21.

36. Scaduto, *Bob Dylan*, 185; Martin Scorsese, *Rolling Thunder Revue: A Bob Dylan Story* (Grey Water Park Productions, Sikelia Productions, 2019).

Dylan's *Rolling Thunder Revue* performance of "Hard Rain," "Bob Dylan 'Hard Rain' LIVE performance [Full Song] 1975 | Netflix," https://www .youtube.com/watch?v=iUD5snx-XOo, retrieved December 23, 2019.

37. I love the way Bruce Springsteen puts it: "Look, you're in a car, your new selves can get in, but your old selves can't get out. . . . The child from 1950, he doesn't get out. The teenager, the adolescent boy, no one can get out. They are with you until the end of the ride." "Springsteen's State of the Union," interview with Jon Stewart, *Rolling Stone*, March 29, 2012.

38. "*Broadside* magazine asked Phil Ochs, another 'protest' singer-songwriter, if he thought that Dylan would like to see his protest songs 'buried.' Ochs replied insightfully: 'I don't think he can succeed in burying them. They're too good. And they're out of his hands.' " Peter Drier, "The Political Bob Dylan," *Huffington Post* (blog), May 25, 2016, https://www .huffingtonpost.com/peter-dreier/the-political-bob-dylan_b_10134862. html, retrieved December 10, 2017. Greil Marcus, "Story of a 'bad song,'" acknowledges that "Masters of War" had a life of its own, independent of whatever may have been Dylan's intention.

39. New York Post, "Jim Carrey and Other Stars Share Updates from Hawaii Following Ballistic-Missile False Alarm," January 14, 2018, https://www .foxnews.com/entertainment/jim-carrey-and-other-stars-share-updates -from-hawaii-following-ballistic-missile-false-alarm, retrieved December 19, 2019. "People across the state were terrified. Many assumed they would die, but sought shelter anyway. They took cover in mall bathrooms, bathtubs, drug stores—even a storm drain. Hawaii has very few shelters, and houses with basements are rare. There were reports of people speeding down highways and running red lights to reunite with family members. Others called one another to say 'I love you' one last time." Alia Wong, "Pandemonium and Rage in Hawaii," *The Atlantic*, January 14, 2018, https://www.theatlantic.com/international/archive/2018/01/pande -monium-and-rage-in-hawaii/550529/, retrieved January 8, 2020.

40. "Chimes of Freedom," on *Another Side of Bob Dylan*.

41. Charukesui Ramadurai, "Shillong: The Indian Town Obsessed with Bob Dylan," *The Independent*, May 22, 2007, https://www.independent.co.uk /travel/asia/bob-dylan-birthday-24-may-shillong-meghalaya-rock-city -lou-majaw-dylan-cafe-a7745176.html, retrieved December 20, 2019.

42. Rita Gatphoh, Shillong (Meghalaya, India), November 11, 2017, recorded by Alessandro Portelli; email to the author, January 13, 2020. "Sur Ka Mariang" ("Tunes of Nature"), composed by Rida Gatphoh and Peter

Marbaniang. Performed by Rida & the Musical Folks, https://www.you
tube.com/watch?v=eCyIjpvea-k, retrieved January 12, 2020.

43. Ananya Ghosh, "I Am Not a Fan of Bob Dylan: Lou Majaw," *Hindustan Times*, https://www.hindustantimes.com/i-am-not-a-fan-of-bob-dylan-lou-majaw/story-Ib5rWTH7bIWMnt3aqdTnuN.html, retrieved December 20, 2019.

44. "Blowin' in the Wind," https://www.youtube.com/watch?v=DIJqa5mOnrc; "Knockin' on Heaven's Doors," https://www.youtube.com/watch?v=81iH-BWvIE; "Mr. Tambourine Man," https://www.youtube.com/watch?v=4vOsXwVAeFE, all retrieved December 10, 2017.

45. Paul Simon and Art Garfunkel, "The Sound of Silence," on *Sounds of Silence* (Columbia, 1966).

46. Paul J. Robbins interview, *L.A. Free Press*, 1965, in Jonathan Cott, ed., *Bob Dylan: The Essential Interviews* (New York: Wenner, 2006), 40. According to Wikipedia, "Quilling or paper filigree is an art form that involves the use of strips of paper that are rolled, shaped, and glued together to create decorative designs. The paper is rolled, looped, curled, twisted and otherwise manipulated to create shapes which make up designs to decorate greetings cards, pictures, boxes, eggs, and to make models, jewelry, mobiles etc." *Wikipedia*, https://en.wikipedia.org/wiki/Quilling. For the Bob Dylan Café and an image of *Dylan a la Quilled*, see https://www tripadvisor.co.nz/LocationPhotoDirectLink-g503702-d9778808-i28552 5873-Dylan_s_Cafe-Shillong_East_Khasi_Hills_District_Meghalaya .htm, retrieved September 21, 2021.

47. The story of the interview is told in Indira Chawdhury's blog, *The Oral Historian*, https://theoralhistorian.com/2020/11/16/a-story-with-no-ending-meeting-vincent-stone, retrieved September 14, 2021. For the region's complicated political and ethnic history, see Sanjoy Hazarika, *Strangers No More: New Narratives from India's Northwest* (New Delhi: Aleph 2018).

48. "Rainy Day Women 12 & 35" on *Blonde on Blonde* (1966). "People . . . draw conclusions on the walls" is from "Love Minus Zero/No Limit" on *Bringing It All Back Home* (1966). On Shillong's drug scene, see TNN, "Drug abuse on the rise in Meghalaya," *Times of India*, https://timesofindia .indiatimes.com/city/shillong/Drug-abuse-on-the-rise-in-Meghalaya /articleshow/54302225.cms, retrieved December 20, 2019.

49. "Most Likely You Go Your Way (And I Go Mine)," on *Blonde on Blonde*.

50. John Cohen and Happy Traum interview, *Sing Out!* October–November 1968, in Cott, *The Essential Interviews*, 125. In a piece released in 2020, at the time of the Covid-19 crisis, Dylan, however, identifies with Blake (along with another slate of poets and historical characters): "I sing the songs of experience like William Blake," "I Contain Multitudes" on *Rough and Rowdy Ways* (Columbia, 2020).

51. Walter J. Ong, *Orality and Literacy: The Technologizing of the Word* (London: Routledge, 2002).

52. Leonard Cohen, "A Singer Must Die," on *New Skin for an Old Ceremony* (Columbia, 1974).

1. SONGS OF INNOCENCE AND EXPERIENCE

1. Quoted in Costantino Nigra's seminal *Canti popolari del Piemonte*, eds. Franco Castelli, Emilio Jona, and Alberto Lovatto (1888; Turin, Italy: Einaudi, 2009), 186. Nigra, a scholar and diplomat in early Italian independence, writes that "the presence of this song in Italy since no less than two centuries was noted by Alessandro D'Ancona as far back as 1874" (unless otherwise noted, all translations from the Italian are mine). D'Ancona noted that the song's first lines had been quoted in a collection of popular songs published in 1629 in Verona by the Florentine artist Camillo, nicknamed Bianchino, and later reproduced in Oskar Ludwig Bernhard Wolff's *Egeria* (1829). D'Ancona also pointed out that the song was mentioned in Lorenzo Panciatichi's 1656 *Cicalata in lode della Padella e della Frittura* (A mock lecture in praise of fried fish and frying pan): *Scritti vari di Lorenzo Panciatichi raccolti da Cesare Guasti* (1856), https://archive .org/stream/bub_gb_s__gBozh77YC/bub_gb_s__gBozh77YC_djvu.txt, retrieved September 21, 2021.

2. Giovanni B. Bolza, *Canzoni popolari comasche* (1866), quoted in Nigra, *Canti popolari del Piemonte*, 186. I first heard Sandra Mantovani's abridged folk revival recording of Bolza's version of the song as "Il testamento dell'avvelenato" in *Il testamento dell'avvelenato: Antiche ballate e canzoni dell'Italia settentrionale* (45 EP, Ricordi, 1963). Mantovani recorded the full text in a later album, *Servi baroni e uomini* (Albatros, 1970). A similar version, collected in the same area by Cristina Melazzi and Riccardo Schwamenthal on March 10, 1974, can be heard on *Regione Lombardia— Documenti della Cultura Popolare—7—Como*, ed. Roberto Leydi (Albatros, 1976), sung by Teresa Tacchini.

3. Clinton Heylin, *Revolution in the Air: The Songs of Bob Dylan Vol. 1: 1957–73* (London: Constable, 2010), 113.

4. Francis James Child, *The English and Scottish Popular Ballads* (1882–1888; New York: Dover, 1965), 1: 182.

5. Jeannie Robertson, title track of the album *Lord Donald* (Collector Records, 1960).

6. Giovanna Risolo, Otranto (Puglie), August 8, 1968. Recorded by Gianni Bosio and Clara Longhini, in Gianni Bosio and Clara Longhini, *1968 Una ricerca in Salento: Suoni, grida, canti, rumori, storie, immagini* (Lecce, Italy: Kurumuny, 2007), 185–87 and CD 1, tr. 17.

7. Carmela Luci, from Molochio, Calabria, recorded by Alessandro Portelli, Rome, October 28, 1973. The original recording is archived in Circolo Gianni Bosio—Archivio Sonoro "Franco Coggiola" (CGB-AFC) Alessandro Portelli Collection, REL 100. Another recording of the same singer by Marco Müller, May 26, 1974, is in CGB-AFC, Marco Müller Collection, MUL005.

8. Bob Dylan writes, "Harry [Belafonte] was the best balladeer in the land and everybody knew it. He was a fantastic artist, sang about lovers and slaves—chain gang workers, saints and sinners and children." *Chronicles: Volume 1* (2004; London, Sydney, New York: Pocket Books, 2005), 68. Dylan recalls several African American songs from Belafonte's repertoire but does not mention "Lord Randal."

9. Jean Ritchie, "Lord Randal," on *British Traditional Ballads from the Southern Mountains, Volume 2* (Folkways, 1961). Dylan mentions Jean Ritchie as one of the folk singers who, unlike Joan Baez, "didn't translate well to a modern crowd." Dylan, *Chronicles*, 254.

10. Giovanna Nobili, "Il testamento dell'avvelenato," recorded by Maria Antonietta Arrigoni and Marco Savini, 2005, on the CD accompanying the 2009 Einaudi edition of Nigra's *Canti popolari del Piemonte*.

11. "Patti Smith performs Bob Dylan's 'A Hard Rain's A-Gonna Fall' - Nobel Prize Award Ceremony 2016," https://www.youtube.com/watch?v=941PHEJHCwU, retrieved December 14, 2017.

12. Alessandro Carrrera, *La voce di Bob Dylan: Una spiegazione dell'America* (Milan: Feltrinelli, 2011), 313.

13. The closest comparison is in Christopher Ricks, *Dylan's Visions of Sin* (2003; New York: Harper Collins, 2016), 357. Ricks's comments on "Hard Rain" are more innovative and to the point than those on "Lord Randal."

14. "L'Orazione di San Donato" ("Saint Donato's death prayer"), recorded by Cesare Bermani at Zaccheo (Teramo, Abruzzi), February 7, 1965, on the album *Italia: Le stagioni degli anni '70*, ed. Alessandro Portelli (Dischi del Sole, 1972). Giovanna Marini's rewriting "Lamento per la morte di Pasolini" on the 1975 murder of poet and filmmaker Pier Paolo Pasolini can be heard on Giovanna Marini's *Antologia* (AlaBianca-Dischi del Sole, 1996).

15. "When you play music by ear it don't mean you wiggle your ears while you're playing it. You sort of write down a bunch of sounds in your mind and save them for future use. Sometimes you hear a tune and catch some of the words, and for a long time you go around with it roaring through your head like a lost steamboat." Woody Guthrie, "Ear Players," *Common Ground* 2, no. 3 (Spring 1942): 32–43. https://www.unz.com/print/CommonGround-1942q1-00032/Contents/, retrieved December 24, 2019. "What happens is, I'll take a song I know and simply start playing it in my head. That's the way I meditate. . . . while I'm driving a car or talking to a person or sitting around or whatever. People will think they are talking to me and I'm talking back, but I'm not. I'm listening to the song in my head. At a certain point some of the words will change and I'll start writing a song." Bob Dylan in Robert Hillburn interview, *Los Angeles Times*, 2004, in *Bob Dylan: The Essential Interviews*, ed. Jonathan Cott (New York: Wenner, 2006), 467. "I never waste my high-priced time by asking or even wondering in the least whether I've heard my tune in whole or in part before. There are ten million ways of changing any tune around to make it sound like my own. I can sing a high note instead of a low note or a harmony note for a melody note and put in a slow note for several fast ones or put in several fast ones for a slow one, and shuffle my rests and my pauses around here and yonder and be able to make the bottom idea of any tune fit my new ballad idea." Woody Guthrie, "Union Maid" (1948), in *Born to Win*, ed. Robert Shelton (New York: Collier, 1967), 82–83. "I changed words around and added something of my own here and there. Nothing do or die, nothing really formulated, all major chord stuff, maybe a typical minor key thing. . . . You could write twenty or more songs off one melody by slightly altering it. I could slip in verses or lines from old spirituals or blues. That was okay; others did it all the time." Dylan, *Chronicles*, 228.

16. Ishmael Reed, *Mumbo Jumbo* (1972; New York: Avon, 1978), 202. Moses does not realize that Jethro has not taught him everything he knows: when he performs the songs in concert, it ends in disaster and rebellion.

17. Eric Lott, *Love and Theft: Blackface Minstrelsy and the American Working Class* (Urbana: University of Illinois Press, 1993).
18. Sean Wilentz, *Bob Dylan in America* (New York: Anchor, 2011), 215.
19. Quoted in Wilentz, *Bob Dylan in America*; brackets and italics in text.
20. See Greil Marcus's review of Dylan's *The Bootleg Series Vol. 8*, "The Bootleg Series Vol. 8: Tell-Tale Signs—Rare and Unreleased 1989–2006," *Barnes and Noble Review*, October 7, 2008, https://www.barnesandnoble.com/review/the-bootleg-series-vol-8-tell-tale-signs-rare-and-unreleased-1989-2006, retrieved January 8, 2020.
21. Pete Seeger, *A Link in the Chain* (Legacy, 1966).
22. Walt Whitman, *Leaves of Grass* (1855), Section 24.
23. Rolling Stone, *100 Greatest Bob Dylan Songs*, https://www.rollingstone.com/music/lists/100-greatest-bob-dylan-songs-20160524/a-hard-rains-A-Gonna-fall-1963-20160523, retrieved January 1, 2018. *Rolling Stone* ranks "Hard Rain" as Dylan's second-best song, after "Like a Rolling Stone."
24. Gordon Hall Gerould, *The Ballad of Tradition* (1932; New York: Oxford University Press, 1957), 3.
25. As we have seen, "Il Testamento dell'avvelenato" and "Lord Randal" are documented in writing in Verona in 1629 and in Edinburgh in 1710, respectively. This, however, is not how Carmela Luci, Jeannie Robertson, and generations of traditional singers learned it and passed it on, keeping it alive.
26. Ewan MacColl, "Lord Randal," on *The Long Harvest: Some Traditional Ballads in their English Scots and North American Variants* (Argo, 1967) , track B1, CD version track 10.
27. Werner Sollors, *Beyond Ethnicity: Consent and Descent in American Culture* (New York: Oxford University Press, 1986).
28. Chimes Freedom, "A Hard Rain, Lord Randall, and the Start of a Revolution," http://www.chimesfreedom.com/2014/12/16/a-hard-rain-lord-randall-and-the-start-of-a-revolution/, retrieved December 24, 2019. This piece mentions the connection to "Lord Randal" and states but does not demonstrate that Dylan's song is a conversation between a father and a son. Alessandro Carrera connects "A Hard Rain's A-Gonna Fall" to the e. e. cummings poem "Buffalo Bill's," which Dylan had known since he was a teenager: "how do you like your blue-eyed boy / Mister Death." Here, the blue-eyed boy may be either Buffalo Bill or Jesus. Carrera, *La voce di Bob Dylan*, 221. As Carrera notes, Dylan's eyes are also blue.

29. "Highway 61," on *Highway 61 Revisited* (1965). In a rare and interesting variant of "Il testamento dell'avvelenato" collected in Puglia from Giovanna Risolo by Gianni Bosio and Clara Longhini, the father is present but the power figure is the son. The mother asks him what he will leave his father and he replies "le lascio di nuovo la corona alla testa," "I leave him the crown back on his head"—as if the father had been divested of all authority as long as the son was alive. Gianni Bosio and Clara Longhini, *1968 Una ricerca in Salento: Suoni, grida, canti, rumori, storie, immagini* (Lecce, Italy: Kurumuny, 2007).

30. In contemporary imagination, even Sir Launcelot is blue-eyed: he is described as blue-eyed in several contemporary novels, like Victor C. Brice's *PenDRAGON's Requite: King Arthur Triumphant* (Bloomington, IN: iUniverse, 2007), 64, or Nathan Neuharth, *King Arthur's Court* (Night Horse, 2017), 172. Hollywood casts the blue-eyed Franco Nero as Sir Launcelot in the 1967 iteration starring Franco Nero and Vanessa Redgrave (Joshua Logan, *Camelot*, Warner Bros.-Seven Arts, 1967).

31. William Coyle, *The Young Man in American Literature: The Initiation Theme* (New York: Odyssey Press, 1969). Dylan, however, was also becoming aware, through Allen Ginsberg and Arthur Rimbaud, of William Blake's *Songs of Innocence and of Experience* (1794), which he later quotes in "Visions of Joanna" on *Blonde on Blonde* (1966) and in "I Contain Multitudes," on *Rough and Rowdy Ways* (Columbia, 2020).

32. "Bob Dylan's Dream" on *The Freewheelin' Bob Dylan* (1963); "Forever Young" (1973) on *Planet Waves* (1974).

33. Ralph Waldo Emerson, "Nature" (1836), in *Essays and Lectures* (New York: Library of America, 1983), 10.

34. "I'd come out of the dark, demonic woods." Dylan, *Chronicles*, 14.

35. Nathaniel Hawthorne, *The Scarlet Letter*, in *The Portable Hawthorne*, ed. Malcolm Cowley (New York: Viking, 1979), 337.

36. The Staple Singers, *Faith and Grace: A Family Journey 1953–1976* (Royal, 2015), record 3; Jimmy Cliff, *Sacred Fire EP* (Collective Sounds, 2011).

37. Bruce Springsteen, "Black Cowboys," on *Devils and Dust* (Sony, 2005); Bill De Blasio, "Transcript: Mayor de Blasio Holds Media Availability at Mt. Sinai United Christian Church on Staten Island," http://www1.nyc.gov/office-of-the-mayor/news/542-14/transcript-mayor-de-blasio-holds-media-availability-mt-sinai-united-christian-church-staten, retrieved December 11, 2015.

38. Bruce Springsteen, "American Skin," on *Live in New York City* (Sony, 2001).

39. "Maria Rossi" (pseudonym), former student activist, quoted in my "I'm Going to Say It Now: Interviewing the Movement," in *The Battle of Valle Giulia: Oral History and the Art of Dialogue* (Madison: University of Wisconsin Press, 1997), 195.

40. Paolo Pietrangeli (1945), film maker and folk singer, interviewed by Alessandro Portelli, Rome, May 28, 1996. Pietrangeli is speaking about the events on March 1, 1968, when for the first time the students, attacked by the police, fought back. "Relatively" here means as compared to the violence that came later.

41. Alessio Aringoli (1978), student, interviewed by Susanna Trifiletti, Rome, June 28, 2002.

42. Brunella Pinto (1981), student, interviewed by Alessandro Portelli, Rome, February 17, 2002. Generations in Genoa, July 2001," *Forum for Anthropology and Culture*, 4 (2007), 346-67.

43. Dylan, *Chronicles*, 18.

44. Steven Mayers and Jonathan Freedman, eds., *Solito, Solita. Crossing Borders with Youth Refugees from Central America* (Chicago: Haymarket, 2019), 107, italics in the text.

45. Images of migrants at Ventimiglia can be seen at https://www.irishtimes.com/news/world/europe/eu-remains-divided-on-migrants-as-italy-struggles-with-influx-1.2251955, https://www.theguardian.com/world/2018/jun/17/italy-ventimiglia-migrants-stuck-at-border-crisis-suffering,https://www.cnn.com/2018/06/15/europe/oxfam-report-migrants-ventimiglia-intl/index.html, all retrieved September 21, 2021.

46. "We tried to escape, but they had helicopters, dogs, and guns." Pedro Hernández (Guatemala), in Mayers and Freedman, *Solito, Solita*, 166. For an image of two white border patrol officers walking a black dog, https://www.alamy.com/stock-photo/border-patrol-dog.html, retrieved September 14, 2021.

47. Mayers and Freeman, *Solito solita*, 102–3. The *hielera* (icebox) is the term used by detainees to refer to cold and damp detention facilities.

48. "*I came here for a good life, and I'm in jail,*" Pedro Hernández in Mayers and Freeman, *Solito, Solita*, 167; italics in text. "When I came I believed that Italy would become my second homeland and that we would be allowed documents that would make me equal to the people who live here." Geedi Kuule Yusuf, recorded by Alessandro Portelli at the Asinitas

school of Italian as a second language, December 16, 2010 (CGB-AFC Portelli Collection—Fondo Musiche Migranti), on the CD *Istaranyieri*, ed. Enrico Grammaroli and Alessandro Portelli, transcribed and trans. Ubax Cristina Ali Farah (Rome: Circolo Gianni Bosio, 2011).

49. https://www.statista.com/statistics/1082077/deaths-of-migrants-in-the -mediterranean-sea/ retrieved September 15, 2021.

50. Rashid, interviewed by Cecilia Bartoli, Rome, spring 2015, in *Calendario civile: Per una memoria laica, popolare e democratica degli italiani*, ed. Alessandro Portelli (Rome: Donzelli, 2017), 262.

51. "Everybody I met seemed to be a rank stranger / No mother or dad not a friend could I see / They knew not my name and I knew not their faces / I found they were all rank strangers to me." The Stanley Brothers, "Rank Stranger," on *The Stanley Brothers: The Early Years 1958–1961, Volume 3* (King Records, 1993). Bob Dylan's rendition of "Rank Stranger to Me" appears on *Down in the Grove* (1988). Dylan performed this song in concert twenty-six times between 1988 and 2001.

52. Geedi Kuule Yusuf on *Istaranyieri*. Translation by Ubax Cristina Ali Farah.

53. Abubakar, Somali migrant, twenty-one years old, interviewed by Dagmawi Ymer at the Castelnuovo di Porto migrant shelter, *Lo straniero*, 264 (February 2014). "They tried to kill me psychologically." Jhony Chuc (Guatemala), in Mayers and Freedman, *Solito, Solita*, 92. Later in the interview, Geedi plays on this word to give a capsule definition of colonialism: Italians came to Somalia as *ospiti* (guests) and stayed as *ospiti* (landlords), turning Somalis into *ospiti* (guests) in their own country.

54. Bob Dylan, "Chimes of Freedom." See also Agnes "Sis" Cunningham's memorable line: "They tell ya to keep moving, but migrate you mustn't do." "How Can You Keep on Moving" on *Sundown* (Folkways, 1976).

55. In May 2021, Mousa Balde from Gambia was badly beaten in the streets of Ventimiglia by three Italian men who accused him of trying to steal a cell phone. As a response, he was taken into custody and locked in a migrant detention center in Turin, where he committed suicide. He was twenty-three years old. And brown-eyed. "Massacrato di botte da tre italiani, si suicida nel CPR di Corso Brunelleschi," *La Stampa* (Turin daily paper), May 23, 2021, https://www.lastampa.it/torino/2021/05/23 /news/massacrato-di-botte-da-tre-italiani-si-suicida-nel-cpr-di-corso -brunelleschi-1.40306059, retrieved June 15, 2021.

56. "Le anime in trappola," composed and sung by Jajit Raj Mehta (immigrant from India), Pontirolo (Cremona, Lombardy), August 15, 2015, recorded by Claudio Piccoli and Piadena Culture League; "We Are Not Going Back," recorded by Andrea Satta, Ventimiglia (Liguria), July 2015, both on the CD *We Are Not Going Back: Musiche migranti di resistenza, orgoglio e memoria*, ed. Alessandro Portelli (Nota-Circolo Gianni Bosio, 2016). Bob Dylan: "Knockin' on Heaven's Door," on *Pat Garrett and Billy the Kid* (1973); "Tryin' to Get to Heaven," on *Time Out of Mind* (1973).

2. THE TEXT AND THE VOICE

1. Roman Jakobson and Petr Bogatyrev, "Folklore as a Special Form of Creation," trans. John M. O'Hara. *Folklore Forum* 13, no. 1 (1980): 1–21.
2. Betsy Miller, interviewed by Alan Lomax, June 12, 1951, http://research .culturalequity.org/get-audio-detailed-recording.do?recordingId=7804, retrieved January 22, 2018. Walter Scott wrote: "I think it not impossible, that the ballad may have originally regarded the death of Thomas Randolph, or Randal, earl of Murray, nephew to Robert Bruce, and governor of Scotland. This great warrior died at Musselburgh, 1332, at the moment when his services were most necessary to his country, already threatened by an English army." *Minstrelsy of the Scottish Border* (1838; London: Thomas Tegg, 1839), 256, 4, 2021, https://deriv.nls. uk/dcn23/8060/80600435.23.pdf, retrieved September 24, 2021. William Langland's *Piers Plowman* (1377) mentions a ballad of Randof (or Ranulf), Earl of Chester, along with the earliest known mention of the Robin Hood ballad cycle: "I do not know my Paternoster / perfectly as the priest sings it / but I know rhymes of Robin Hood /and Randolf Earl of Chester." No text of the ballad survives; Langland probably refers to Ranulf III, Earl of Chester. James W. Alexander, however, suggests that the connection with Robin Hood indicates that the song may have been an outlaw ballad. In this case, the hero may have been Ranulf de Gernons IV, Earl of Chester, a "more likely candidate for the role of rebel against authority," who died (like Robin Hood), "reportedly of poison by William Peverell of Nottingham, possibly assisted by [his] own wife." James W. Alexander, "Ranulf III of Chester: An Outlaw of Legend?" *Neuphilologische Mitteilungen* 83, no. 2 (1982): 152–57. There is, however, no evidence that "Lord Randal" may have been sung in Scotland before it was mentioned in Italy in 1629: Francis James Child notes that of "the

[English and Scottish] versions that have come down to us . . . none . . . can be traced back further than a century." *The English and Scottish Popular Ballads* (1882–1888; New York: Dover, 1965), 1: 152, https://www.jstor .org/stable/43343443.

3. Daniel Bertaux and Martin Kohli, "The Life Story Approach: A Continental View," *Annual Reviews of Sociology* 10 (1984): 215–37. Here and elsewhere in this book, I use "text" in quotes in the sense defined by Jurij Lotman and Boris Uspenskij, "On the Semiotic Mechanism of Culture," *New Literary History* 9, no. 2 (Winter, 1978): 211–32.

4. The two versions of "Il Testamento dell'avvelenato" sung by Carmela Luci and recorded by me in October 1973 and by Marco Müller in May 1974 are far from identical. Several vernacular expressions found in the first version are replaced by more standard Italian forms in the second (e.g., "cacciato," Southern vernacular for "served," becomes the more standard "portato"); in the second version, the singing style is more conventional, with a sort of bel canto finale. All this suggests that Carmela Luci, a Southern farm worker who migrated to the urban periphery of Rome, found herself in a fluid, uncertain cultural position, between the memory of her folklore heritage and the incompletely mastered linguistic and artistic norm. She was also probably more self-conscious as an artist and performer after she was "discovered," and may have tried to embellish her performance the next time she was asked. There are other textual variations that have to do with memory: in the latter performance, Carmela Luci forgets the verse in which the hero's mother asks him to make his will and adds a verse about what he will leave his brother that she had omitted the first time; she also repeats twice the verse about the lover's punishment, once in the wrong place.

5. Dennis Tedlock, "The Spoken Word and the Work of Interpretation in American Indian Religion," in *The Spoken Word and the Work of Interpretation* (Philadelphia: University of Pennsylvania Press, 1983), 236.

6. "Dove sei stato, mio bell'alpino" ("Where have you been, my handsome *alpino?*" [the Alpini were Army units of mountain infantry]), see Franco Castelli, Emilio Jona, and Alberto Lovatto, *Al rombo del cannon: Grande Guerra e canto popolare* (Vicenza, Italy: Neri Pozza, 2018), 253–54; for "Billy Boy" as a variant of "Lord Randal," Peggy Seeger, on *The Long Harvest, Volume. 1* (Argo, 1966); Frank Howes, *Folk Music of Britain—and Beyond* (London: Methuen, 1969), 114.

7. Mark Brown, "Bob Dylan's early draft for A Hard Rain's A-Gonna Fall shows telling changes," *The Guardian*, August 24, 2015, https://www .theguardian.com/music/2015/aug/24/bob-dylan-early-draft-for-a-hard -rains-a-gonna-fall-shows-telling-changes, retrieved January 22, 2018. Apparently, however, there is more than one "original" manuscript.

8. Cecil J. Sharp, *English Folk Song: Some Conclusions* (1907; East Ardsley, Wakefield, UK: EP Publishers, 1965), 16.

9. See Greil Marcus's comments on Pete Seeger's live performance, in *Bob Dylan: Writings 1968–2010* (New York: Public Affairs, 2011), 60. Bob Dylan, on the other hand, says that "[his] songs really aren't meant to be covered." Paul Zollo interview, *Song Talk*, 1991, in *Bob Dylan: The Essential Interviews*, ed. Jonathan Cott (New York: Wenner, 2006), 397. Only in exceptional cases another artist may turn a song into a completely different work of art: see Jimi Hendrix's appropriation of Dylan's "All Along the Watchtower" on *Electric Ladyland* (Reprise, 1968).

10. "A Hard Rain's A-Gonna Fall," bobdylan.com/songs/hard-rains-gonna-fall, retrieved January 14, 2018.

11. A fan's comment on Dylan's St. Paul, July 10, 2013 concert. Other comments take contrasting views: "Holy crap. He sounds so horrible! It's sad to watch"; "It's the patina of years that enhances the experience. Like good wine that gets better over the years"; "It's like watching Picasso paint in front of your eyes"; "He sounds like the cookie monster." https://www.youtube.com/watch?v=KwI7b5Lm6bg&index=3&list =RDcxeDR9m_25I, retrieved September 15, 2021. On the other hand: "Dylan will always be Dylan as Dylan is today. Meaning, to go see him is to go see Dylan today. The guy has always changed and has always been unpredictable": Michael Lello, "An Interview with the Beets," April 16, 2013, http://highway81revisited.com/an-interview-with-the-beets/, retrieved September 15, 2021.

12. For a fuller discussion, see my *The Text and the Voice: Speaking, Writing and Democracy in American Literature* (New York: Columbia University Press, 1994).

13. Mikal Gilmore interview, *Rolling Stone*, December 22, 2001, in Cott, *The Essential Interviews*, 350; see also, Betsy Bowden, *Performed Literature: Words and Music by Bob Dylan* (Bloomington: Indiana University Press, 1989).

14. Commenting on Dylan's live performance of "The Lonesome Death of Hattie Carroll," Christopher Ricks notes, "He cannot re-perform

the song. He unfortunately still does. There is no other way of singing this song than the way in which he realizes it on 'The Times They Are A-Changin'.' If he sings it any more gently, he sentimentalizes it. If he sings it any more urgently, he allies himself with [Hattie Carroll's murderer] William Zantzinger." Ricks later partly revised this judgment. Christopher Ricks, *Bob Dylan's Visions of Sin* (New York: Ecco, 2004), 16 ff.

15. Andrea Cossu, "Down the Foggy Ruins of Time: Bob Dylan and the Performance of Timelessness," in *Tearing the World Apart: Bob Dylan and the Twenty-First Century*, ed. Nina Goss and Eric Hoffman (Jackson: University Press of Mississippi, 2017), 53.

16. "Bob Dylan—Tangled Up in Blue (Live 1984)," https://www.youtube.com/watch?v=jeBC7svBhfo, retrieved January 23, 2018; Bob Dylan, *Real Live* (1985).

17. "A Hard Rain's A-Gonna Fall—New Orleans 2003," https://soundcloud.com/micheleulysse/02-a-hard-rains-A-Gonna-fall; "A Hard Rain's A-Gonna Fall—St. Paul, MN—July 10, 2013," https://www.youtube.com/watch?v=KwI7B5Lm6Bg&index=3&list=RDcxeDR9m_25I, both retrieved January 23, 2018; "Bob Dylan's 'Hard Rain' LIVE Performance [Full Song] 1975," https://www.youtube.com/watch?v=i-UD5snx-XOo, retrieved October 15, 2019. See also Martin Scorsese's *Rolling Thunder Revue: A Bob Dylan Story*, (Grey Water Park Productions, Sikelia Productions, 2019). For a version of "Hard Rain" with slight changes to the melody but only a very minor one ("before I start sinking" instead of "until") to the words, see *The Bootleg Series No. 7: No Direction Home* (2005).

18. Vienna Di Lorenzo, Buonacquisto (Terni, Umbria), August 10, 1974; Angiola Pitari, Fornole (Terni), February 13, 1977; Ada Barbonari and Rosa Scorsolini, Castellonalto (Terni), January 20, 1978. Recorded by Valentino Paparelli, archived in Circolo Gianni Bosio—Archivio Sonoro (CGB-AFC), Paparelli collection, vP74.9, 77.3, 78.2.

19. In 1765, Bishop Thomas Percy was already presenting folk songs as *The Reliques of Ancient English Poetry* (1765). Many of them lived on for centuries afterward.

20. Mark Edwards and Lloyd Timberlake, *Hard Rain: Our Headlong Collision with Nature* (London: Still Pictures Moving Words, 2009); see also, Hard Rain Project, http://www.hardrainproject.com/d, retrieved January 5, 2018.

21. Walter J. Ong, *Orality and Literacy: The Technologizing of the Word* (New York: Routledge, 2002).

22. See Gianni Bosio, "Elogio del magnetofono: Chiarimento alla descrizione dei materiali su nastro del fondo Ida Pellegrini" (1970) ("In praise of the tape recorder: Clarification of the description of the materials on tape of the Ida Pellegrini Fund") in *L'intellettuale rovesciato* (Milan: Istituto Ernesto de Martino/Jaca Book, 1998), 157–66.

23. "A woman like you should be at home / That's where you belong," "Sweetheart Like You," on *Infidels* (1983). In a way, this song can be heard as a gender-inverted variant of "Hard Rain"; the innocent young woman leaves "[her] father's mansion" and wanders into a "dump," a literal waste-land.

24. Frank Proffitt, on *North Carolina Songs and Ballads* (Topic Records, 1966); Colum McDonagh, on *The Folk Songs of Britain Volume 4: The Child Ballads—1* (Topic Records, 1969); Betsy Miller and Ewan McColl, on *A Garland of Scots Folksong* (Camsco, 2009).

25. For Teresa Viarengo, see *Il cavaliere crudele* (Dischi del Sole, 1965); *Teresa Viarengo e la ballata popolare in Piemonte* (Nota, 1998).

26. Original spellings of "Parliamentry" and "aegin'" were retained.

27. "All Along the Watchtower" (Bob Dylan's official website dates this song as 1968, but it appears in the 1967 album *John Wesley Harding*). In a creative misunderstanding, the graffiti changed Dylan's "the princes" to "the princess" and illustrated it with the drawing of a captive princess gazing into the distance from her tower.

28. "Songs like 'Which Side Are You On?' . . . they're not folk-music songs; they're political songs. They're *already* dead." Bob Dylan, Nat Hentoff interview, *Playboy*, March 1966, in Cott, *The Essential Interviews*, 105. Like Mark Twain, however, Dylan can be quoted on both sides of each issue. A moment earlier, in the same interview, he said that "There's nobody that's going to kill traditional music." Perhaps his contrast between "traditional" and "political" derives from the fact that he still didn't realize that even the "folk" live "in a political world" (Bob Dylan, "Political World," 1989, on *Oh Mercy*). Traditional musicians also vote and sometimes go on strike and sing about it (putting, like Florence Reece in this case—and like Dylan himself—new words and subjects to traditional tunes). He was wrong about "Which Side Are You On?" anyway. In the third millennium, "Which Side Are You On?" was far from dead: the Occupy Wall Street movement gave it new life by using

it as all folk songs are used, inventing new verses and lines, adapting it to the time and the place. This is how it was sung in the streets and later recorded by Ani DiFranco on *Which Side Are You On?* (Righteous Babe Records, 2012). DiFranco opens the track by sampling the guitar chords from Pete Seeger's classic version. The song was alive and flexible enough to be used in the civil rights movement (The Freedom Singers, on *Sing for Freedom. The Story of the Civil Rights Movement through Its Songs* [Smithsonian Folkways, 1990]) and by the striking maritime workers in Sidney, Australia (Mark Gregory, "Join the MUA", on *With These Arms: Songs and Poems of the MUA* [Maritime Union of Australia, 2003]). During the 1984–1985 British miners' strike, it was retrieved, changed, and used by Billy Bragg (Billy Bragg—"Which Side Are You On?," https://www.youtube.com/watch?v=vbddqXib814, retrieved October 15, 2019) and by the Scottish folk singer Dick Gaughan (*True and Bold*, Scottish Trade Union Congress, 1984). In 2008, it was recorded by Natalie Merchant on *The House Carpenter's Daughter* (Myth America, 2008); on a YouTube post, Merchant's version is opened by the voice of the song's author, Florence Reece, who was also not dead when she sang "Which Side Are You On" for striking Harlan miners in 1973 and at the great union demonstration in Washington in 1982, sixteen years after it had been proclaimed dead by Bob Dylan. The standard recording of the song is Pete Seeger's with the Almanac Singers, *Talking Union* (1941; Folkways, 1955 and Smithsonian Folkways, 2004). On the song's origin and background, see my *They Say in Harlan County: An Oral History* (New York: Oxford University Press, 2010), 235–36.

29. "*Hok Kolorob* Lyrics Arnob," https://www.youtube.com/watch?v =ogtCuP6CQa4. On the song's impact on the student movement at Kolkata, see Deviyot Goshal, "A Brief History of #*Hok Klorob*, the hashtag that shook Kolkata," *Quatz India*, October 9, 2014, https://qz.com /india/269774/hokkolorob-the-hashtag-thats-defining-an-indian -student-protest-against-violence/, both retrieved June 19, 2021.

30. Sourav Saha, Jadavpur University, Kolkata (India), November 16, 2016. Echoes of Bob Dylan's "It's All Right, Ma (I'm Only Bleeding)," (on *Bringing It All Back Home* [1965]). Professor Indira Chodhury explains: "Eklavya was a Nisadh—a tribal and hence not a high caste youth. But he was a great archer who was difficult to defeat and his guru had demanded that he sacrifice his thumb so that Prince Arjuna could be declared the best archer. The story of a highly skilled low caste man

defeated by trickery has resonances for the Dalit movement and is often re-interpreted in India today when we talk about tribals or low caste persons being cheated and deprived of what is rightly theirs" (email to the author, January 20, 2020).

31. "Amra Korbo Joy", performed by Sanchari Sangeetayan, Bengali music and dance school, directed by Sushmita Sultana, recorded by Alessandro Portelli, Rome, February 2, 2016, on *We Are Not Going Back: Musiche migranti di resistenza, orgoglio e memoria*, ed. Alessandro Portelli (Nota-Circolo Gianni Bosio, 2016).

32. Sourav Saha, December 20, 2017. The *pujapandal* is a temporary structure for the performance of a *puja*, a worship ritual for a godhead. *Durgapuja* is the holiday of the goddess Durga.

33. Ewan MacColl, "Lord Randal," on *The Long Harvest* (Argo, 1967).

34. Gordon Hall Gerould, *The Ballad of Tradition* (1932; New York: Oxford University Press, 1957), 3.

35. For a discussion, see my "The Time of My Life: Functions of Time in Oral History," in *The Death of Luigi Trastulli and other Stories: Form and Meaning in Oral History* (Albany, NY: SUNY Press, 1981), 59–76.

36. Gerould, *The Ballad of Tradition*, 4–5.

37. *Live at the Gaslight 1962* (2005); "Gaslight 1961," https://www.youtube .com/watch?v=95N1rFtC7-E, retrieved January 8, 2020. Bob Dylan used the tune of "Pretty Polly" in "The Ballad of Hollis Brown" (1963, on *The Times They Are A-Changin'*) and in the banjo riff in "High Water" (2001, on *"Love and Theft"*).

38. See my article *Los usos del olvido*, in *Histórias Orales: Narración, imaginación, diálogo* (Rosario, Argentina: Prohistoria, 2016), 485–99.

39. In the booklet accompanying record 2 of *The Long Harvest: Some Traditional Ballads in their English Scots and North American Variants* (Argo, 1967).

40. Albert B. Lord, *The Singer of Tales* (Cambridge, MA: Harvard University Press, 1960).

41. Tony Atwood, " 'A Hard Rain's A Gonna Fall': The Meaning of the Lyrics and the Music" (2015), http://bob-dylan.org.uk/archives/1550, retrieved April 12, 2017; Studs Terkel interview, in Cott, *The Essential Interviews*, 6.

42. For an early instance of enjambement in Dylan's work, listen to "Motorpsycho Nightmare" (1964, on *Another Side of Bob Dylan*): "He said he's going to kill / Me if I don't get out the door."

43. Alessandro Carrera, *La voce di Bob Dylan: Una spiegazione dell'America* (Milan: Feltrinelli, 2011), 144.

44. I discuss how this process takes place in oral history interviews in "*Absalom, Absalom!*: Oral History and Literature", in *The Death of Luigi Trastulli*, 270–82.

45. A list: *S*tumbled on the *s*ide; *m*isty *m*ountains; *C*rawled on six *c*rooked highways; *M*iles in the *m*outh; *S*even *s*ad fore*s*ts; A *d*ozen *d*ead oceans; *W*ild *w*olves; *B*lack *b*ranch with *b*lood; *T*en thousand *t*alkers whose *t*ongues; A *w*ave that could dro*w*n the *w*hole *w*orld; *H*eard one *h*undred drummers *w*hose *h*ands; A *c*lown who *c*ried; A *w*hite man who *w*alked a black dog; *b*ody was *b*urning; *W*ho *w*as *w*ounded; The *d*epths of the *d*eep*est* black for*est*; *P*ellets of *p*oison; *D*amp *d*irty prison; *St*and on the ocean until I *st*art *s*inkin'; My *s*ong well before I *st*art *s*ingin'.

46. Giovanna Risolo, in Gianni Bosio and Clara Longhini, *1968 Una ricerca in Salento: Suoni, grida, canti, rumori, storie, immagini* (Lecce, Italy: Kurumuny, 2007): "what do you leave your sisters . . . I leave them a full dowry / What will you leave your coachmen . . . I leave them my coach / What will you leave your father . . . I leave him the crown back to his head."

47. "Jimmy Randal," as performed by Emma Hensley, Carmen, North Carolina, and by Peggy Seeger on *The Long Harvest*, B2: tr. 11.

48. F. B. Gummere, *The Popular Ballads* (London-Boston-New York: Constable/Houghton Mifflin, 1907), 101–3.

49. Bob Dylan probably knew "Lonesome Valley" from a Carter Family recording (a reprint is on *The Famous Carter Family*, Harmony, 1970); he heard it from Joan Baez and Mary Travers at the 1963 Newport Folk Festival. Dylan quotes the song in "Tryin' to Get to Heaven," on *Time Out of Mind* (1997): "I've been walking that lonesome valley trying to get to heaven before they close the door."

50. "Maggie's Farm," on *Highway 61 Revisited* (1965).

51. For instance, in verse 2: *son, one, around it, on it, drippin', a–bleedin', broken, children*—and the last: *fallen, prison, hidden, forgotten, sinkin', singin'*. As if they were there to prepare us for the *rain* at the end.

52. "King Henry," in Francis James Child, *The English and Scottish Popular Ballads* (1882–1888; New York: Dover, 1965), 160; Harry Belafonte, "Lord Randal," on *The Best of Belafonte*, (RCA, 1956); Ada Barbonari and Rosa Scorsolini, CGB-AFC, vP 78.2: "gallows to hang her, fire to burn her, rope to choke her."

53. Sean Wilentz, *Bob Dylan in America* (New York: Anchor, 2011), 69. On Dylan and the Beats, see chapter 2, "Penetrating Aether," 47–84.

54. Robert Cantwell, *When We Were Good: The Folk Revival* (Cambridge, MA: Harvard University Press, 1997), 345.

55. "Baby Face" was written in 1926 by Harry Akst and Benny Davis; it is included on Little Richard's 1957 album, *Here's Little Richard* (Specialty, 1957). In his high school years, Bob Dylan listened to Little Richard and performed his songs in his early public appearances. Anthony Scaduto, *Bob Dylan* (New York: Grosset & Dunlap, 1971), 6–12.

56. Wilentz, *Bob Dylan in America*, 66. "Someone gave me a book of François Villon poems and he was writing about 'hard-core street stuff' and making it rhyme. . . It was pretty staggering and it made you wonder why you couldn't do the same thing in a song. I'd see Villon talking about visiting a prostitute and I would turn it around. I won't visit a prostitute, I'll talk about rescuing a prostitute." Robert Hilburn interview, in Cott, *The Essential Interviews*, 463.

57. Folksinger Dave Van Ronk, quoted in Carrera, *La voce di Bob Dylan*, 70.

58. Carrera, *La voce di Bob Dylan*, 313.

59. Carl Sandburg, *The American Songbag* (New York: Harcourt Brace, 1927). "It was Sandburg, in fact, who captured Dylan's imagination. The Illinois populist represented the flip side of his endless fascination with Woody Guthrie." Douglas Brinkley interview, *Rolling Stone*, May 14, 2009, in Cott, *The Essential Interviews*, 510. In 1964, Dylan visited Sandburg at his home and gave him a copy of *The Times They Are A-Changin'*.

60. Bob Dylan and Allen Ginsberg's *Holy Soul Jelly Roll*, recorded in 1971 (Rhino Records, 1994).

61. Ricks, *Dylan's Visions of Sin*, 115.

62. The "dying prophet-poet" is sung in a well-known anarchist song, Pietro Gori's "Inno al Maggio" (May Day Anthem, 1892); a version from oral tradition, recorded by Franco Coggiola at Filo d'Argenta (Emilia), May 1, 1965, is on *Italia: Le stagioni degli anni '70* (1972; Ala Bianca-Dischi del Sole, 1979). Google gives 1,760,000 occurrences for "weeping clown"; perhaps the most familiar is in Ruggero Leoncavallo's opera *I Pagliacci* (1892).

63. "Poets drown in lakes . . . Poets usually have very unhappy endings. Look at Keats's life. Or Jim Morrison, if you want to call him a poet." Paul Zollo interview, *Song Talk*, 1991, in Cott, *The Essential Interviews*, 392, 396. Perhaps Dylan was not thinking of Keats but of Shelley, dead by water like the hero of "Hard Rain."

3. TALKING ATOMIC BLUES

1. Bob Dylan, Studs Terkel interview, in *Bob Dylan: The Essential Interviews*, ed. Jonathan Cott (New York: Wenner, 2006), 7.
2. Alan Lomax, Pete Seeger, and Woody Guthrie, eds. *Hard-Hitting Songs for Hard-Hit People*, foreword by John Steinbeck (New York: Oak, 1967).
3. Bob Dylan, "Barbara Allen" (Francis James Child, *The English and Scottish Popular Ballads* [1882–1888; New York: Dover, 1965], no. 84), on *Live at the Gaslight* (2005); "A recording from that time [early 1960] of him singing the traditional ballad 'Barbara Allen' tears at the heart strings." Suze Rotolo, *A Freeewheelin' Time. A Memoir of Greenwich Village in the Sixties* (New York: Broadway Books, 2008), 183. "Scarlet Town" is on *Tempest* (2012). See Jochen Markhorst, "Bob Dylan's Fascination with Barbara Allen," https://bob-dylan.org.uk/archives/9788, retrieved May 3, 2021.
4. Joan Baez, "What Have They Done to the Rain," written by Malvina Reynolds, *Joan Baez in Concert* (Vanguard, 1962); Malvina Reynolds, *Held Over* (Cassandra Records, 1967); Marianne Faithfull, *Marianne Faithfull* (Decca, 1965). For "Little Boxes," see Pete Seeger, *We Shall Overcome* (Columbia, 1963); Malvina Reynolds, *Malvina* (Cassandra Records, 1977).
5. Alessandro Carrera, *La voce di Bob Dylan: Una spiegazione dell'America* (Milan: Feltrinelli, 2011), 310–25.
6. Nat Hentoff interview, in Cott, *The Essential Interviews*, 29, 30.
7. Bob Dylan, *Chronicles: Volume 1* (2004; London, Sydney, New York: Pocket Books, 2005), 29, 30.
8. Bob Dylan, "With God Our Side," from *The Times They Are a-Changin'* (1964).
9. Bob Dylan, "Ye Playboys and Playgirls," with Pete Seeger, on *Newport Broadside* (Vanguard, 1964).
10. Jeff Place and Ronald D. Cohen, eds. *The Best of Broadside 1962–1968: Anthems of the American Underground from the Pages of Broadside Magazine* (Washington, DC: Smithsonian Folkways, 2000), 41.
11. Mark Spoelstra, "The Civil Defense Sign," on *The Best of Broadside Vol. 1* (Folkways, 1963), CD 2. On Dylan and Spoelstra as a performing duo, see Suze Rotolo, *A Freewheelin' Time: A Memoir of Greenwich Village in the Sixties* (New York: Broadway, 2008), 13.

12. Quoted in Jean-Michel Guesdon and Philippe Margotin, *Bob Dylan All the Songs: The Story Behind Every Track* (New York: Black Dog & Leventhal, 2015), 189.

13. "Let Me Die in My Footsteps," with Happy Traum on *Broadside Ballads, Volume 1* (Folkways, 1963); solo, on *The Bootleg Series, Volume 1* (1991) and *The Bootleg Series Vol. 9—The Wittmark Demos:1962–1964* (2010).

14. Pete Seeger, "I Come and Stand at Every Door" (from Nazim Hikmet's "Hiroshima Child"), on *I Can See a New Day* (Columbia, 1964). Joan Baez sings "The Great Seal of Shule Skerry" as "Silkie" on *Joan Baez, Vol. 2* (Vanguard, 1961). Peggy Seeger and Ewan MacColl's "There's Better Things for You" is on *New Briton Gazette, Volume 1* (Folkways, 1960).

15. Ishiji Asada and Koki Kinoshita, "Genbaku o yurusumaji." The song was written in 1954 for the first meeting of the united Japanese anti-nuclear movement (until then, divided between Socialists and Communists), held in Hiroshima in 1955 (Sara Park, University of Kobe, email to the author). Pete Seeger learned it from Ewan MacColl's English translation and sings it in Japanese on the album *Rainbow Quest* (1960; Smithsonian Folkways, 2004). Original text and a translation can be found at https://www.antiwarsongs.org/canzone.php?lang=it&id=934, retrieved January 2, 2018.

16. Odetta sings Alex Comfort's "One Man's Hands" on *It's a Mighty World* (RCA, 1964). Nina Simone adapted another British anti-nuclear ditty, Matt McGinn's "Go Limp," to the non-violent resistance tactics of civil rights movement by changing CND to NAACP. "Go Limp" is the story of a young woman who has learned that when the police arrest her at a demonstration, she must "go limp" and not resist. When a young man comes courting her, she applies the same tactic, and does not resist. In the end, she explains to her mother: "There's no need for distress / That marcher has left me / His name and address / And if we win / Though a baby there be / He won't have to march / Like his da-da and me." Matt McGinn's performance of "Go Limp" is in *The Best of Broadside 1962–1988*, 34–35 and on CD 1; Nina Simone's adaptation is on *Nina Simone in Concert* (Philips, 1964).

17. Nina Simone's classic rendition of the spiritual "Sinnerman" shares the apocalyptic vision of Dylan's "Hard Rain." The sinner seeks refuge in the river and the sea, but they are bleeding and boiling, there is no refuge. Nina Simone, "Sinnerman," on *Pastel Blues* (Philips, 1965).

18. Jann S. Wenner interview, *Rolling Stone*, 2007, in Cott, *The Essential Interviews*, 486. Dylan here says that *Modern Times* is also about the bomb's cultural impact. There is, however, no explicit mention of it in the album's lyrics.

19. "Itsy Bitsy Teenie Weenie Yellow Polka Dot Bikini" was a hit for Brian Hyland in 1960. Yellow and black were the colors of the civil defense signs for the air raid shelters. See my "Atom Bomb Baby: la musica e la bomba da Hiroshima a Bob Dylan," *Linea d'ombra*, December 17, 1986, 72–77. The Five Stars' "Atom Bomb Baby" and Sheldon Allman's "Radioactive Mama" and many more like them are collected on *Atomic Platters: Cold War Music from the Golden Age of Homeland Security* (Bear Family, 2014).

20. Golden Gate Quartet, "Atom and Evil" (1947) on *Atomic Café: A Soundtrack Album* (Rounder, 1982). Several of the songs discussed here are also reissued in *Atomic Platters*.

21. Sam Hinton, "Talking Atomic Blues," on *Newport Broadside* or *Atomic Platters*.

22. Vern Partlow, "Talking Atomic Blues," on *The Folk Box* (Elektra, 1966). For writing this song, according to his Wikipedia page, Vern Partlow was fired, blacklisted, and investigated by the FBI, https://en.wikipedia.org/wiki/Vern_Partlow, retrieved May 3, 2021.

23. Buchanan Brothers, "Atomic Power" (1946) and Karl Davis and Harty Taylor, "When the Atom Bomb Fell" (1946), both on *Atomic Café* and *Atomic Platters*.

24. "Things Have Changed" (1989), on the soundtrack of the Curtin Hansom film *Wonder Boys* (Columbia/Sony Music Soundtrax, 2000) and *The Essential Bob Dylan* (Columbia, 2000).

25. Harry Belafonte, "Come Away Melinda," written by Fran Minkoff and Fred Hellemarn, on *Streets I Have Walked* (RCA, 1963). In the same year, the song was also recorded by Judy Collins, *Judy Collins #3* (Elektra, 1963) and The Weavers, *Reunion at Carnegie Hall Part 1* (Vanguard, 1963).

26. Bill Haley and His Comets, "Thirteen Women (And Only One Man in Town)," written by Dickie Thompson (1954), on *Bill Haley's Greatest Hits*, (Coral, 1969; German release) and *Atomic Platters*. "Thirteen Women" was the B side of Bill Haley's historic "Rock Around the Clock."

27. "Talkin' World War III Blues," on *The Freewheelin' Bob Dylan* (1963).

28. Don DeLillo, *Underworld* (1997; London: Picador, 1998), 76.

29. Fintan O'Toole, *Irish Times*, quoted in http://www.hardrainproject.com/d, retrieved December 7, 2019.

30. Mark Edwards and Lloyd Timberlake, *Hard Rain: Our Headlong Collision with Nature* (London: Still Pictures Moving Words, 2006); see also *Hard Rain Project: Roadmap to a Sustainable Future*, http://www.hard rainproject.com/film, retrieved December 7, 2019. The image of the oil-soaked cormorant was used by U.S. propaganda during the war in Iraq, though it came from an entirely different context. Ethics and Quality, "Fakes in Journalism," *European Journalism Observatory*, https://en.ejo.ch/ethics-quality/fakes-in-journalism, retrieved December 27, 2019.

31. Barbara Plett, "Bob Dylan song adopted by Copenhagen climate summit," *BBC News*, http://news.bbc.co.uk/2/hi/8396803.stm, retrieved January 5, 2018.

32. Gino Martina, "Taranto: un fiume rosso lungo le strade vicino all'Ilva: 'Qui il vento e la pioggia fanno paura," *La Repubblica*, Bari edition, November 14, 2017, https://bari.repubblica.it/cronaca/2017/11/14/news/taranto_un_fiume_rosso_lungo_le_strade_del_porto_vicino_all_ilva_qui_il_vento_e_la_pioggia_fanno_paura_-181123051/, retrieved September 17, 2021.

33. "Acid rain" contains pollutants like sulphur and nitrose oxides derived from fossil fuels: YPTE – Young People's Trust for the Environment, *Acid Rain. What is It?*, https://ypte.org.uk/factsheets/acid-rain/forests, retrieved 12.7.2019; D.R.I. (Dirty Rotten Imbeciles), *Acid Rain on Live* (Rotten Records, 1994); Peter Gabriel, "Red Rain", on So (Charisma, 1986).

34. Bob Rivers, "Acid Rain," on *Twisted Tunes—Seattle vol. 2* (Collectorz, 1995). In an obvious double entendre, "Acid rain will fade your car and kill your grass / Still the President is kissing . . . babies."

35. Avenged Sevenfold, "Acid Rain," on *Hail to the King* (Warner Bros., 2013); Reagan Youth, "Acid Rain" (1983), on *The Complete Youth Anthems for the New Order* (New Red Archives, 2017).

36. Amitav Ghosh, *The Great Derangement: Climate Change and the Unthinkable* (Chicago and London: University of Chicago Press, 2016), 52.

37. Woody Guthrie, "The Great Dust Storm" (1940), on *Dust Bowl Ballads* (Smithsonian Folkways, 2004). The song is based on another disaster ballad, "The Sherman Cyclone," which Woody Guthrie learned from his mother.

38. Charlie Patton, "High Water Everywhere" (1929), on *The Definitive Charlie Patton* (Catfish, 2001).

39. Bessie Smith, "Back Water Blues" (1927), on *The Bessie Smith Story, Volume 4* (Columbia, 1951); Mahalia Jackson, "Didn't It Rain," on *Gospels*,

Spirituals & Hymns (Columbia, 1991); Louis Armstrong, *Louis and the Good Book* (RCA, 1958); Bob Dylan, *Bob Dylan Live at Carnegie Hall, New York City, November 4, 1961* (Columbia, 2005).

40. The Carter Family, "No Depression in Heaven" (1936), on *More Favorites by the Carter Family* (Ace of Hearts, 1966); Tom Morello, "Midnight in the City of Destruction," on *The Fabled City* (Epic, 2008).

41. Memphis Minnie, "When the Levee Breaks" (1929), on *Blues Classics— Memphis Minnie* (Blues Classics, 1964).

42. Bob Dylan, "High Water (for Charley Patton)," on *"Love and Theft"* (2001) and "The Levee's Gonna Break," on *Modern Times* (2006). On the subject of broken levees, we may remember Bruce Springsteen's post-Katrina version of Blind Alfred Reed's "How Can a Poor Man Stand Such Times and Live," on *We Shall Overcome. The Seeger Sessions* (Columbia 2006). "There's bodies floating on Canal and the levees gone to hell . . . them who's got, got out of town / and them who ain't got left to drown." Yet, an always hopeful Bruce Springsteen also sings that "We stood the drought, now we'll stand the rain." "Jack of All Trades," on *Wrecking Ball* (Sony, 2011).

43. Murray Leeder and Ira Wells, "Dylan's Floods," *Popular Music and Society* 32, no. 2, (2009): 211–27; Alessandro Carrera, "La pioggia alla fine del tempo: Bob Dylan tra simbolismo e modernismo," *Acoma. Rivista internazionale di studi nordamericani* 26, no. 9 (Spring, 2003): 104–15. "Crash on the Levee" is on *The Basement Tapes* and, as "Down in the Flood," on Dylan and The Band's double live album *Before the Flood* (Asylum, 1974).

44. Ernesto de Martino, *La fine del mondo. Contributo all'analisi delle apocalissi culturali*, ed. Clara Gallini (Turin, Italy: Einaudi, 2002), 479–80.

45. Blind Lemon Jefferson, "Rising High Water Blues," on *Blind Lemon Jefferson* (Milestone, 1961).

46. Vito Teti, *Quello che resta: L'Italia dei paesi, tra abbandoni e ritorni* (Rome: Donzelli, 2017), 152–53, 169; Ian Chambers, *Mediterraneo blues: Musiche, malinconia postcoloniale, pensieri marittimi* (Mediterranean blues: music, melancholy, sea visions) (Turin, Italy: Bollati Boringhieri, 2010). I am thinking also of the sense of displacement in another kind of "Mediterranean blues"; "I run from the animals that bear arms / I am no longer African, I am not Italian—What are we all?": Geedi Yusuf's song of migration, title track of the CD, *Istaraniyeri*, eds. Alessandro Portelli and Enrico Grammaroli (Circolo Gianni Bosio—Provincia di Roma, 2011).

47. Bob Dylan, "Señor (Tales of Yankee Power)," on *Street Legal* (1978).

48. Lincoln County may be the county in New Mexico that was the scene of the last gunfight between Pat Garrett and Billy the Kid, narrated in the Sam Peckinpah film for which Dylan wrote the soundtrack (*Pat Garrett and Billy the Kid*, 1973). In this case, the song might be about the alternative between two typologically related wars. Or, as suggested by Robert Shelton (quoted in Alessandro Carrera's notes to the Italian edition of Bob Dylan, *Lyrics 1969–1982* [Milan: Feltrinelli, 2016], 446) it might be Lincoln County Road, the road that leads to Jimmy Carter's plantation, which Dylan visited in 1974; in this case, the alternative would be between politics and the apocalypse (though Carter is the only politician to whom Dylan was not completely hostile, it is hard to believe that for him politics may be a way of salvation rather than another form of Disaster).

49. Bob Dylan and The Band, "Crash on the Levee (Down in the Flood)," on *The Basement Tapes*.

50. Studs Terkel interview, in Cott, *The Essential Interviews*, 8.

51. Genesis 28:10–17; John 1–51. Some of the most memorable renderings of "We Are Climbing Jacob's Ladder" are those of Paul Robeson, Pete Seeger, and Bruce Springsteen. Joan Baez and Bob Gibson combine it with another spiritual, "We Are Crossing Jordan River," at the 1959 Newport Folk Festival (*Folk Festival at Newport*, NotNow, 2011).

52. Bob Dylan, "God Knows," on *Under the Red Sky* (1990). Dylan probably knew "God Gave Noah the Rainbow Sign" from the Carter Family (on *The Original and Great Carter Family*, RCA, 1962) and may be citing it in "Desolation Row" (*Blonde on Blonde*, 1966); "though her eyes are fixed upon Noah's great rainbow / She spends her time peeking into Desolation Row." James Baldwin, "The Fire Next Time" was published in 1963. On floods and rains in Bob Dylan's songs, see Leader and Wells, "Dylan's Floods."

4. WHICH WAY HISTORY?

1. Emily Dickinson, in *The Poems of Emily Dickinson*, ed. Ralph W. Franklin (Cambridge, MA: Harvard University Press, 1998), no. 1263

2. Zygmunt Bauman, *Memories of Class: The Pre-History and After-Life of Class* (1982; London: Routledge & Kegan Paul, 2009), 1–2.

3. Carlo Ginzburg, "Introduzione," in *Il filo e le tracce* (Milan: Feltrinelli, 2006), 10–11, translation mine.

4. Carlo Ginzburg, "Morelli, Freud and Sherlock Holmes: Clues and Scientific Method," *History Workshop*, No. 9 (Spring, 1980), 5–36.

5. Rodney Hilton, *Bond Men Made Free: Medieval Peasant Movements and the English Rising of 1381* (London: Temple Smith, 1973), 114.

6. Bauman, *Memories of Class*, 42–43 (bracketed italics mine); Gerald Porter, "Melody as a Bearer of Radical Ideology: English Enclosure, *The Coney Warren* and Mobile Clamour," in *Rhythms of Revolt: European Traditions and Memories of Conflict in Oral Culture*, eds. Eva Guillorel, David Hopkins, and William G. Pooley (London: Routledge, 2018), kindle edition loc. 5910–6538.

7. Vito Teti, *Quel che resta: L'Italia dei paesi, tra abbandoni e ritorni* (Rome: Donzelli, 2017), 6. On "Fior di Tomba" (Nigra 19) and "Bella ciao", Roberto Leydi, *La canzone popolare - 1. La possibile storia di una canzone, in Storia d'Italia*, vol. 5 (Turin, Italy: Einaudi, 1973), 1183-1197; Cesare Bermani, *La "vera" storia di Bella Ciao*, "Il de Martino", Sesto Fiorentino, n. 8, 1998, pp. 49-87. Bessie Smith, "In the House Blues", on *Bessie Smith - The Complete Recordings vol. 4* (Columbia, 1991); Lightnin' Hopkins, "Woke Up this Morning", on *Down Home Blues* (Bluesville, 1964); Robert Johnson, "Me and the Devil Blues", on *The Complete Recordings*, Columbia, 1990; B. B. King, "Woke Up This Morning" (1953; *A Proper Introduction to B. B. King*, Proper Records, 2004).

8. The song is well known in Italy but is most popular in the Italian community in Brazil; I heard it in an Italian restaurant in Caxias, Rio Grande do Sul, a town still identified with Italian immigration. The version I quote here comes from Elisa Benigni, from Ranica (Bergamo, Lombardy), recorded in 1980, as performed by Sandra and Mimmo Boninelli in *"Il bastimento parte . . ." I canti dell'emigrazione bergamasca* (Edizioni Junior, 1996).

9. Recorded by Alessandro Portelli, Rome, July 15, 2011, on *We Are Not Going Back: Musiche migranti di resistenza, orgoglio e memoria*, ed. Alessandro Portelli (Nota-Circolo Gianni Bosio, 2016).

10. Italia Ranaldi home recording, Circolo Gianni Bosio—Archivio Sonoro (CGB-AFC), Italia Ranaldi collection, ITR 001.

11. *Mamma mia dammi cento lire* is based on the ballad *La maledizione della madre* (Nigra 23, "the mother's curse"), in which the young woman elopes with a knight who turns out to be the devil. In *The Daemon Lover or The House Carpenter* (Child 24), a carpenter's wife leaves her family to elope with a beau who turns out to be the devil, and sinks in the the sea,

sometimes in view of Italy. Bob Dylan performed *The House Carpenter* early in his career (see *The Bootleg Series volume 1*); he may refer to it in *Tangled Up in Blue*: some people "we used to know … are mathematicians, some are carpenters' wives." Or he was thinking of the wife of Joseph the carpenter ("Must be the Mother of our Lord", *Duquesne Whistle*, on *Tempest*). The Devil or God? "It may be the devil or it may be the Lord, but you're gonna have to serve somebody" : *Gotta Serve Somebody from Slow Train Coming* (1980).

12. Many other songs voice the sense of loss caused by emigration and the resentment against those who leave: "there's no one left here anymore but priests and friars, nuns, and few desperate merchants . . ." ("Italia bella mostrati gentile," as sung by Tullio Fati, Fossombrone [Marche], November 1972, recorded by Dario Toccaceli, CGB-AFC, Toccaceli collection 019); or, "my husband has gone to America and isn't writing, I wonder what I did wrong—perhaps what I did wrong was that he left me with three daughters and now he has four … ": **Marìtema églie sciut'a la Mèreca,** in Beniamino Tartaglia, *Documenti orali di Aquilonia (già Carbonara)* (Aquilonia, Avellno province: Museo Etnografico di Aquilonia, 2005) no page number. Or the Neapolitan classic, "Lacreme napulitane," ("How many tears is America costing us Neapolitans") (Libero Bovio—Francesco Bongiovanni, 1925); for a classic rendition, Roberto Murolo, "Lacreme Napulitane—Remastered" https://www.youtube.com/watch?v=Hqrp4In18ao . See my " 'Non ci rimane più che preti e frati.' Appunti sui canti contro l'emigrazione," (notes on anti-emigration songs), in *Stranieri nel ricordo. Verso una memoria pubblica delle migrazioni*, ed. Daniele Salerno and Patrizia Violi (Bologna, Italy: Il Mulino, 2021), 19–40.

13. Luciano Gallino, *La lotta di classe dopo la lotta di classe* (Bari, Italy: Laterza, 2012).

14. "Kelly, The Boy from Killane," written by P. J. McCall, in James N. Healy, *The Second Book of Irish Ballads* (Cork, Ireland: Mercier, 1962), 100–102.i; see The Clancy Brothers and Tommy Makem, *The Rising of the Moon: Irish Songs of Rebellion* (Tradition, 1959). Shelmalier is a place in Wexford County where some of the events of the 1798 uprising took place; the "guns of the sea" may refer to the French expeditions that landed in Ireland to support the Irish rebellion.

15. Ian Watson, *Song and Democratic Culture in Britain* (London-New York: St. Martin's, 1983), 66–67, 76, and passim. For Filippo Turati's "Canto dei lavoratori," see *Avanti Popolo alla riscossa—Antologia della canzone*

socialista in Italia (Dischi del Sole—Ala Bianca, 1996); for "Fischia il vento," see *Pietà l'è morta—Canti della Resistenza italiana 1* (Dischi del Sole—Ala Bianca, 1989). "You don't need a weatherman / To know which way the wind blows," Bob Dylan, "Subterranean Homesick Blues" on *Bringing It All Back Home* (1965).

16. Ernesto de Martino, *Morte e pianto rituale nel mondo antico* (1958; Turin, Italy: Bollati Boringhieri, 2008).

17. Jorge Luis Borges, "El jardín de senderos que se bifurcan" (1941), in *Ficciones* (1944; Barcelona, Spain: Seix Barral, 1986).

18. Woody Guthrie, "Gypsy Davy" (1944), on *The Asch Recordings, Volume 1* (Smithsonian Folkways, 1999).

19. Alessandro Carrera, *Note del traduttore*, in *Bob Dylan: Lyrics 1983–2012* (Feltrinelli Editore, 2017), 449. Dylan probably knew "Matty Groves" (Child 81) through Joan Baez (*Joan Baez in Concert Part 1* [Vanguard, 1962]). "Henry Lee," a version of "Love Henry" (Child 86) performed by Dick Justice, is the first track on Harry Smith's Folkways *Anthology of American Folk Music*, a key source for the young Bob Dylan, who sings it (as "Harry Lee") on *World Gone Wrong* (1993). In "Barbara Allen" (Child 84), the heroine rejects Sweet William, who dies for love of her; she repents, dies for love in turn, and the two are buried next to each other. Bob Dylan recorded "Barbara Allen" in 1962 on *Live at the Gaslight 1962* (2005).

20. Jean Ritchie, *Ballads from Her Appalachian Family Tradition* (Smithsonian Folkways, 2003); Vance Radolph, *Ozark Folksongs* (Columbia: University Press of Missouri, 1946–1950).

21. "Cecilia" (Nigra 3), Gallerana Orsini (Polino, Terni), June 3, 1973, recorded by Valentino Paparelli and Alessandro Portelli; Luigi Matteucci and Benedetta Baldorossi (Polino, Terni), December 29, 1974, recorded by Valentino Paparelli. Both versions are in *La Valnerina ternana. Un'esperienza di ricerca-intervento*, eds. Valentino Paparelli and Alessandro Portelli (Roma: Squilibri, 2011), 127–35, and on the accompanying CD. The same ambivalence is found between two versions included in anthologies of folk songs from Rome. In Giggi Zanazzo, *Canti popolari di Roma e del Lazio* (1910; Milan: Newton Compton, 1977), the husband encourages Cecilia to submit to the captain's blackmail; in Giuseppe Micheli, *Storia della canzone romana* (1969; Milan: Newton Compton, 2005) he says he'd rather die than allow her to go. In all cases, she accedes to the request of the captain, who in the end betrays her; in most versions, she kills him in

revenge. For a full critical and historical treatment of "Cecilia," see Luisa Del Giudice, *Cecilia: Testi e contesti di una ballata tradizionale* (Brescia, Italy: Grafo, 1996).

22. Aurelio Rigoli, *Scibilia Nobili e altre "storie"* (Parma, Italy: Guanda, 1965).

23. Maria Adorni, Rome, January 31, 2013, recorded by Sara Modigliani, CGB-AFC Other Researchers collection.

24. Julia Scaddon, "The Prickelly Bush," recorded by Peter Kennedy for BBC, on *The Child Ballads No. 1* (Caedmon, 1961) (Child 95).

25. Walter Lucas and his neighbors at Sixpenny Handley, Dorset, "The Pricklie Bush," recorded by Peter Kennedy in 1951, on *World Library of Folk and Primitive Music: England*, ed. Alan Lomax (Rounder, 1998).

26. Huddie Ledbetter, "The Gallis Pole," on *Leadbelly's Last Sessions* (Folkways, 1966); A. L. Lloyd, cover notes to The Watersons, *Green Fields* (Topic, 1981).

27. "Gallows Pole" is on *Led Zeppelin III* (Atlantic, 1970).

28. Giovanni Battista Giraldi Cinthio, *Hecatommithi* (1565). In Shakespeare's play, the sovereign intercedes in the end, saves the hero, and punishes the villain. The folk ballad has a much more pessimistic, and realistic, vision of power.

29. "Anathea," Judy Collins, on *#3* (Elektra, 1963). Written by Neil Roth and Lydia Wood, "Anathea" is a translation of a Hungarian ballad, "Féher Anna," collected by Béla Bartók and included on his *Hungarian Folk Songs*, published in the United States in 1931; S. Gee, "The Price, My Dear, Is You," *Sing Out!* August 17, 2012, https://singout.org/2012/08/17/the-price-my-dear-is-you/, retrieved December 28, 2019. In "Geordie" (Child 209), the hero is to be hanged for stealing one of the king's horses.

30. Bob Dylan, "Seven Curses" (1963) on *The Bootleg Series, Volume 2*. Bob Dylan and Judy Collins had met in 1959, and often performed in the same venues: see Todd Harvey, *The Formative Dylan: Transmission and Stylistic Influences, 1961–1963* (Washington, DC: Scarecrow Press, 2001), 98.

31. Alessandro Carrera, *La voce di Bob Dylan: Una spiegazione dell'America* (Milan: Feltrinelli, 2011), 278. "Golden Vanity" is the title track of a bootleg album, *The Golden Vanity* (Wanted Man, 1992). Dylan performed it seven times in concert from 1991 to 1992.

32. The word "pale" evokes the "pale horse, and its rider's name was Death," Revelations, 6:8. "Pale Horse and Its Rider" is also a song by Hank Williams, an artist that Bob Dylan recalls as his favorite before he discovered

Woody Guthrie Bob Dylan, Chronicles: *Volume 1* (2004; London, Sydney, New York: Pocket Books, 2005), 49.

33. Alessandro Carrera, *La ballata del Nobel: Bob Dylan a Stoccolma* (Milan: Sossella, 2017), 36.

34. Carrera, *La voce di Bob Dylan*, 39.

35. Bob Dylan, "It's All Right, Ma (I'm Only Bleeding)," on *Bringing It All Back Home* (1965).

36. Quoted in David Hajdu, *Positively 4th Street: The Lives and Times of Joan Baez, Bob Dylan, Mimi Baez Fariña, and Richard Fariña* (New York: Farrar Straus and Giroux, 2001), 236.

37. In an excellent essay, Thad Williamson argues that Dylan's later work also evinces a social and political consciousness. Dylan's America, he notes, is a deeply troubled society, marked by the "original sin" of slavery and racism and split by the tragic inequalities of "the existence of suffering," "poverty," "power, powerlessness," and "moral corruption." However, we can literally count on the fingers of one hand the cases in which Dylan names responsibilities or suggests some form of action. His more explicitly "political" songs ("Political World," "Workingman's Blues #2," "Union Sundown") tend to be generic and also less poetically successful. Williamson mentions "Honest with Me" (2001, on *"Love and Theft"*)—a song that seems to allude back to "Restless Farewell," but conveys a sense of an ending rather than a new start: "I'm not sorry for nothin' I've done / I'm glad I fought—I only wish we'd won." Williamson concludes that Dylan clearly shows how suffering and cruelty are pervasive in the modern world and, while he does not call us to act, he invites us to think deeply about the state we are in. Thad Williamson, " 'Everybody 's Got to Wonder What's the Matter With This Cruel World Today': Social Consciousness and Political Commentary in *'Love and Theft'* and *Modern Times*," in *Tearing the World Apart: Bob Dylan and the Twenty-First Century*, ed. Nina Goss and Eric Hoffman (Jackson: University Press of Mississippi, 2017), 158–76.

38. Elisabetta Povoledo, "Italy Arrests Captain of Ship That Rescued Dozens of Migrants at Sea," *New York Times*, June 29, 2019.

39. Sean Wilentz, *Bob Dylan in America*, (New York: Anchor, 2011) 41–43 and Carrera, *La voce di Bob Dylan*, 71. Some textual analogies: "There's a ship, the Black Freighter, with a skull on its masthead, *will be coming in*" and will open fire *"from her bow."* For a memorable performance of "Pirate Jenny," see Nina Simone, *In Concert* (Phillips, 1964).

40. Karl Marx and Friedrich Engels, *The Communist Manifesto* (ebook), http://www.gutenberg.org/cache/epub/61/pg61-images.html, retrieved December 16, 2019.

41. Bob Dylan, *The Bootleg Series No. 7: No Direction Home* (2005).

42. Nevio Brunori (1954), interviewed by Alessandro Portelli, Terni, April 20, 2008; see Alessandro Portelli, *La città dell'acciaio: Due secoli di storia operaia* (Rome: Donzelli, 2017), 289.

APPENDIX: HISTORY'S LESSONS UNLEARNED

1. Bob Dylan, "Murder Most Foul" and "I Contain Multitudes," on *My Rough and Rowdy Ways* (Columbia, 2020).

2. Andy Greene, "Beyond JFK: 20 Historical References in Bob Dylan's 'Murder Most Foul'," *Rolling Stone*, March 27, 2020, https://www.rollingstone.com/music/music-news/bob-dylan-murder-most-foul-jfk-references-974147/ retrieved September 9, 2021.

3. See my *The Text and the Voice: Writing, Speaking and Democracy in American Literature* (New York: Columbia University Press, 1994), 31–37 and passim.

4. There is more than a hint of a conspiracy theory in this song; the taking of Kennedy's brain evokes the autopsy more than the murder itself, and it wasn't Oswald who took over Kennedy's power seat.

5. I explore the Buried King myth in *Il re nascosto: Saggio su Washington Irving* (Rome: Bulzoni, 1979), and "The Buried King and the Memory of the Future: From Washington Irving to Bruce Springsteen," *Memory Studies* 13, no. 3, (2020): 267–276.

6. See my " 'We do not tie in twine': Waste, Containment, History and Sin in Don DeLillo's *Underworld*" in *America Today: Highways and Labyrinths*, ed. Gigliola Nocera (Siracusa, Italy: Grafia, 1993), 592–609.

7. The incident that marked Dylan's departure from the political and musical world of the liberal folk revival—his controversial speech at the Emergency Civil Rights Union's Tom Paine award (followed shortly afterwards by the equally controversial electric performance at Newport) took place in the wake of Kennedy's murder. See "Bob Dylan and the Twenty-First Century," introduction to *Tearing the World Apart: Why Dylan Matters*, eds. Nina Goss and Eric Hoffman (Jackson: University of Mississippi Press, 2017), 5.

8. I thank Alessandro Carrera for pointing out the Vietnam reference in "Charlie." I had been reading it instead as a variant of the "Mr. Charlie"

that Black people used to designate arrogant white men, as in James Baldwin's *Blues for Mister Charlie*. In the polysemy of symbols in this song, the two may not be mutually exclusive.

9. Roosevelt is evoked in the song's second line, in which Dylan refers to November 23, 1963, with the phrase that Roosevelt coined after the attack on Pearl Harbor, December 8, 1942: "a date which will live in infamy."

10. Johnnie H. Robinson, Eddie Ray Zachery, and Group, "Assassination of the President," on *Negro Folklore from Texas State Prisons*, recorded by Bruce Jackson, (Elektra, 1965).

11. Herman Melville, *Moby-Dick; or, The Whale* (1851; Harmondsworth, UK: Penguin, 1992), 126.

12. Pete Seeger, "Where Have All the Flowers Gone?," on *The Bitter and the Sweet* (Columbia, 1962).

INDEX OF NAMES

INDEX OF NAMES

INDEX OF NAMES

INDEX OF NAMES

INDEX OF ALBUMS

INDEX OF SONGS